THE SHORT-GUN MAN

The Code of the West called for settlement of disputes by the Colt 'peacemaker' or short-gun. In a land where every man wore a short-gun it was a brave man indeed who threw down a general challenge. Yet this is exactly what *The Short-Gun Man* did, defying the gunmen whom he thought responsible for perpetuating an injustice.

Men and women were to discover there was no better friend nor more bitter an enemy than he.

OTHER JOHN KILGORE TITLES IN LARGE PRINT

The Man From Secret Valley

THE SHORT-GUN MAN

THE
SHORT-GUN MAN

by
John Kilgore

MAGNA PRINT BOOKS
Long Preston, North Yorkshire,
England.

British Library Cataloguing in Publication Data

Kilgore, John, *1916—*
  The short-gun man.
  Rn: Lauren Paine

  ISBN 1-7505-0000-X

First Published in Great Britain by Robert Hale Ltd, 1962

Published in Large Print 1990 by arrangement with Robert Hale Ltd. London.

Printed and Bound in Great Britain by
Redwood Press Limited, Melksham, Wiltshire.

Chapter One

HARRISON crossed the dry creek-bed with a ground-swelling little wind whipping around his horse's fetlocks and stopped in the first fringe of jack-pines. Summer was nearly gone; the wind had an edge to it and at night each star was diamond-bright and wickedly sharp appearing. There was still heat during the daytime, particularly out on the desert he had just crossed, but it kept receding, rolling back towards the mountains.

Harrison ate jerky and watched his horse nibble among the underbrush. It was pleasant to be sitting stock-still for a change; to be part of the silence, the gradually lengthening shadows and the pine scent.

He made a cigarette looking back over the desert. Nevada, someone had told him, got a lot of rain in the fall. Harrison exhaled watching the little wind send dust-devils writhing out where the alkali was thickest. A lot of folks, he thought, knew a lot about places they had never seen, apparently, for there wasn't anything green as far as he could see except the pine forest at his back and not even jackrabbits ate green pine needles.

He shrugged and went on slouching and smoking, idly seeking movement in the immensity of the desert. It really didn't matter anyway whether Nevada was green in the fall because he wasn't going to stay there. He leaned back finally, let his body run loose in the soft silence, and his face slackened too, the greeny eyes widening a little below Harrison's hat-brim, the full sweep of his jaw settling comfortably into his mood. Nothing mattered much now that he was across the desert. The future was almost as empty as the sky above; almost. One thing he had to do; after that autumn could blow Frank Harrison like a tumbling leaf anywhere it wished, he would not resist.

Lying there like that, Harrison saw the scuffed toes of his boots and the length of legs and thought that no one would ever take him for anything but what he was; a good man with a horse, a rope, and a gun. Funny thing about people; once they'd typed you, why that was what you remained to them. Frank Harrison was a good man with a rope and a horse and a gun; he

8

looked the part. He had a rider's looseness about him and the sun had scorched layers of tan over his face. All his features were rugged and his shape had the flat, honest angularity of a man who makes his living from the saddle.

That, thought Harrison, was very funny, because he had never wanted to be a cowboy and he had never wanted to be a gunfighter either, but people had always typed him as one or the other and he had become both. You drift with the tide, he told himself; you let people make something out of you even if it's something you never particularly wanted to be. The reason you let them do that is simply because you don't know exactly what you want to be, yourself.

He got up, killed the cigarette, dusted off pine needles and caught his horse. Just one more thing to do then he'd become again what the Indians called a "drinker of the wind," a drifter.

When Harrison stepped across the saddle he reined west; the same direction he'd been riding now for many days; west across the last bunched up knuckle of mountains and if the letter in his pocket was correct he should make Pioche about sunset. The horse began picking its way through the trees

9

seeking a buck-trail which would angle upwards. If the horse, like its rider, had not been a stranger in this country it would have known where the trails were.

The important thing though was to take your time. A man could ride a horse almost indefinitely with only grass in him, if he didn't hasten. It was the urge to get somewhere in a hurry that killed horses, particularly in an arid, lethal land like this. Sometimes it also killed men, and when Harrison saw the lazy dust rising from a big burnt-brown meadow up ahead he reined up in the tree-shadows and watched.

It was a horseman; too far off to tell more than that, and he was in a hurry. He was putting his horse along the sidehill in a run. Then Harrison saw him strike a trail and drop down into a loose lope. After that the rider faded in the afternoon murk. Fine; that was what Harrison wanted; a trail. He made for it riding loosely, speculating on what would make a man hurry in these mountains. He'd had nothing else to think about since leaving Colorado thirty days earlier, but the things around him – and the bleak inward thing which stayed close; the thing which had brought him here.

The trail was ankle-deep in dust and

hornflies were as thick as gnats indicating that a drive of cattle had been driven past not too long before. Harrison followed the trail to its summit and part way down the far side. In the west a reddening disc hung off-centre in the sky. There was a village in a long, thin valley down below and a chocolate coloured river that seemed scarcely to move at all. That, he thought, would be the village of Pioche, and the river would be the Muddy. Behind him shadows came stealthily to lay flat fingers of dinginess down the mountainside. Ahead, beyond the long valley, was a limitless wasteland. He thought again of the rain which was supposed to come to Nevada in the fall and grunted. From the looks of things rain didn't soften this country in the fall or any other time.

He whip-sawed down the mountainside following the trail to its levelling off. Now the sun was fast failing and something like dust-smoke settled on the land. Far out on the horizon splintered light reflected skyward from barren upthrusts of solid rock and the sun, punctured by a jagged peak gushed blood-red brilliance briefly, then it began to swiftly fall beyond the mountains drawing away the last light. The coolness increased at once but on this side of the mountains there was no wind. Harrison buttoned his jumper, re-settled his hat with a tugged-forward movement and rode steadily towards Pioche. What a helluva country to settle in, he thought. What could have induced a man to ever write glowing letters about this upended strip of Purgatory anyway; especially a man who had known the full richness of Colorado in the summertime. He made another cigarette, lit it and exhaled without once taking his eyes off the village which was squaring-up closer with dark lines and planes. There began to be a scent of water in the evening; a grass-clover fragrance too and Harrison shrugged. The long narrow valley had looked good from the mountainside; as good as Colorado to be fair about it; but beyond the valley was desolation and behind Harrison for hundreds of miles was more of the same.

Pioche, as Harrison approached it, appeared typical of Western towns except that it had an air of permanence. He thought dryly that anything near water in Nevada was likely to be permanent and anything distant from water would not be permanent. The trail broadened gradually and swung out and around Pioche to approach it from the south and run its full length as the main thoroughfare. Forming shadows showed two rows of buildings one on either side of this roadway and surprisingly enough they stretched northerly for a full four squares. Mostly they were of slab-wood, which he thought must be high-priced in this treeless waste, with a scattering of very old adobes. One building though was of kiln-burnt brick and it was taller than the other buildings. As he passed along the dusty roadway, nearly deserted now at suppertime, he noticed that this was the Meadow Valley Hotel.

Harrison left his horse at the livery stable, took his saddlebags and crossed to the hotel. It cost him a silver cartwheel to get an upstairs room and a quarter more for a bath, then he went forth into the night for a stroll of Pioche and wound up at the Meadow Valley Hotel's dining-room.

He had the layout of Pioche in his mind now and he had appraised the people. Pioche could have been in Colorado or Wyoming or Montana; it was one of those ranch-country towns which environment, Western economy, and necessity, combined to create along every river, each mountain pass, and nearly all the good trails west of Nebraska

13

Territory.

Harrison bought a cigar and smoked it while awaiting his supper. There was an oil-cloth covering on his table and a mug of coffee at his elbow; luxuries to a man who had known only the smell of campfire ashes and horse-sweat for over thirty days. Somewhere beyond the dining-room, out in the night perhaps, rose the rich fluted laughter of a woman. Harrison's head grew still in its swinging study of the room's other occupants; his eyes darkened and his lips around the cigar softened their pressure. That was a sound he had not heard in a long time; a sound that brought up in a rush all the loneliness of the star-studded nights on the trail.

The urges of a man who was often alone in far places always came swiftly to fasten upon a sound like that; next best thing to seeing the woman who made the sound. Harrison did not have long to wait.

When she swept through the doorway and paused for a slow glance at the people in the dining-room Harrison's greeny eyes, slitted against up-curling cigar smoke, closed down upon her with unconcealable hunger. She was young and black-headed with a thrusting fullness of the upper body and a solid completeness which fired every male instinct

14

in him. Then she moved forward ahead of a large man who had stopped to discard his hat and Harrison's eyes never left her. She turned just before sitting at a table and glanced fully into Harrison's face. It was as though something had signalled her from across the room; something that she wasn't certain of and which annoyed her. Harrison saw the smoky flare of her glance and suddenly set-look of her mouth. He did not drop his eyes nor did she. There was a boldness to her gaze; a confidence Harrison could not recall ever encountering in a woman before. She knew she was framed in his sight as being desirable. She also, even at that distance, saw the hunger in him. Then her escort moved the chair, she sat, and the spell was broken.

Harrison turned away finally when his meal came. He ate slowly, appreciatively, and drank four cups of coffee, then sat back and for the first time in many days tiredness came.

Everything a man did was divided into sequences. When one sequence ended and before the next sequence began, there was reaction and anticipation; a period of reflection which, in Frank Harrison's case, took this form. He relaxed fully for perhaps ten full minutes then arose, picked up his hat and crossed to the doorway. There, he turned for a backward glance and met again the unabashed gaze of the smoky-eyed woman. Her escort was eating with relish and saw nothing. Harrison thought he saw a look of interest; but he also saw that certain knowledge in her face which said plainly that she was familiar with the hungers of men. He turned, put on his hat and left the hotel dining-room.

Night was fully down over Pioche and the formless substance of darkness was everywhere. He went forward over the plankwalk and into the dusty roadway bound for the livery stable. There, after seeing that his horse had been rubbed down, hayed and grained, he returned to the roadway, made a second circuit of the town then dropped down on a bench in front of the hotel and thumbed back his hat. A pair of horsemen broke away from a saloon hitchrail and loped easily northward. Their conversation was musical in the night. A spanking-fine team of matched bay horses went past ahead of a dusty top-buggy. Harrison glimpsed the slightly built bearded man who was driving. Two lean shadows materialised out of the gloom across the road, hesitated a moment in front of a saloon then pushed on inside. Harrison raised his eyes and read the over-head sign. THE CATTLEMEN'S CLUB it said; he thought it a good name for a cow-country saloon.

A grizzled man swung past and threw Frank Harrison only a brief glance; then he slowed at the entrance to the hotel, turned and sent back a second glance. Reflected lantern light from each side of the doorway showed off his weathered face and the nickel circlet on his shirtfront. The Marshal seemed interested in Frank's ivory-gripped belt-gun and the low-slung way he wore it.

From the corner of his eye Frank felt this interest. After the lawman had entered the hotel Frank's eyes, deep in shadow, were faintly amused. He got up then, stretched, crossed the roadway and entered The Cattlemen's Club Saloon. It was as he had expected, a popular spot. The letter in his pocket had said it was directly across from the hotel and so far the letter had not been wrong in anything.

He walked to the bar, signalled for a drink and stood sideways gazing at the tables, at the men and girls, and finally at a tall man sitting alone in a far corner with a glass and bottle before him on the table. For

17

many seconds their eyes held, then Frank's drink came, he downed it, dropped a coin and left the saloon without looking again into the dark corner.

He lingered outside long enough to make a cigarette, light it and exhale a bluish cloud, then he walked steadily southward towards the tarpaper shacks he had passed earlier on his way into Pioche.

Behind him a sharp-shouldered silhouette moved easily in the same direction.

Frank kept on going after he had passed the last shack and stopped when he came to a sloping path which meandered off westerly towards the Muddy River. There, he located a grey old deadfall cottonwood and sat upon it, one leg wagging gently. A strong-grinding sound of footfalls came to mingle with the thick lapping of water and Frank put out his cigarette watching up the little trail. The big man came out into the clearing and stopped. He said in a deep-booming voice: "Hello, Frank. You just get in?"

"About dusk," Harrison answered. "How long you been here?"

"Since yesterday."

"Any sign of George?"

The big man came forward and sank down with a head-shake. "Not yet; but he

18

had the farthest to come."

Harrison appraised the large man. He was younger, taller and broader than Frank, but there was a similarity between them. "It's been a long time, Will."

The big man smiled; it made him look even younger, more boyish. "Yeah. You look about the same, Frank. Still punching cows?"

Frank nodded, watching his brother's face and feeling an odd emotion of warmth and gentleness. "You?" he asked.

"The same too," Will Harrison said. "Still a Wells-Fargo guard on the Carson City, San Francisco run."

Frank turned to gaze at the river. "You'd think after six years one of us would start amounting to something, wouldn't you?"

Will Harrison chuckled. "Still fretting aren't you? Well; remember what George used to tell us when we were all home: Take your time, life'll find your place for you."

Frank made no immediate reply. The river looked cleaner at night with star-shine to dilute its stained-coffee surface. "I thought all the way over here that we shouldn't let George come in this, Will."

"Well; why not. After all Jes . . ."

"George's a banker, kid. He's got no call

19

making a play where guns are used. You ought to realise that."

Will Harrison's open, honest face creased into a frown. "It doesn't matter what a man is, Frank. Not when his brother's been killed like Jess was."

That was one thing their father had drilled into them, Frank thought now; they were a family and perhaps even more than that they were pardners; had always been close to one another. Frank Harrison, Will Harrison, George Harrison, and Jess Harrison. Jess was dead now, here in Meadow Valley. He'd had a little ranch somewhere around Pioche. It was all there in the letter in Frank's pocket, except how he had died, and that hadn't even been explained in the marshal's letter which accompanied Jess's personal things back to the home place in Colorado.

"Well," Frank finally said, "George can be a Harrison here in Pioche. You and I'll be strangers with different names."

Will considered this a moment then nodded. "All right; if you think that's the best way."

"I think it is. Will?"

"Yeah."

"Did you find his place?"

20

"I told you I just got here yesterday, Frank."

"All right. I'm going to find out where it was and you hang around town watching for George. When he gets in tell him we're going to be strangers to one another until we find out what was behind Jess's murder."

"I'll tell him."

"An' also tell him to dig up everything he can from the Marshal, and when I get a chance we'll get together."

Chapter Two

ALL his life Frank Harrison had been able to make friends easily and in a strange town the best place to pick up local gossip was always the livery barn. Pioche proved no exception. By the time he got back uptown, though, it was rather late and the day-man was gone. The nighthawk was a young cowboy evidently down on his luck. He nodded up at Frank from a tilted-back chair; his eyes were misted over with something akin to sullenness and his mouth was set in an unpleasant line. Where lantern-light showed, the nighthawk's face was a bright red and his normally pale eyebrows were sun bleached to a straw colour. Frank made a cigarette and slouched; over the rim of paper he studied the cowboy. When he lit up he said, "Getting cool these nights." It was an automatic thing to say; a conversation opener. The nighthawk didn't even nod; he continued to stare out into the empty roadway at nothing. Frank smoked a while before speaking again.

"How long's this valley?" he asked, thinking by a question to force an answer. He was successful.

"Pretty long, mister. Runs all the way from Maopa south of here down in Clark County, up to Pioche. We're at the north end of it."

"Looks like good cattle country, what I've seen of it," said Frank.

The cowboy's mouth drooped. "Yeah; good cow country," he said, and snapped his lips closed for a moment. Frank waited. "Real good cow country, mister. But only in the valley. You go east or west and you got millions of acres of nothin'."

"I came over the east pass today."

"Then you know what's out there. Desert and jack-pinehills. The same west of here."

"You don't sound like you care much about this country," Frank said.

"Care much about it," the nighthawk blurted out. "Dammit mister, I was born here. I'm twenty-two years old and I'm still here. If I didn't like it would I be swamping out a doggoned livery barn?"

"Doesn't seem likely," replied Frank, sensing closeness to the younger man's bitterness. "But you sure don't seem real pleased to me."

"I got reason not to be pleased, mister. Up until two years ago Pioche was about all I'd ask of a town, an' Meadow Valley was better'n anything I'd seen on the outside."

"Then what happened?"

"The Chandlers came here – that's what happened. Luke Chandler and his sister Isabel. Luke calls her Belle."

Frank dropped the cigarette and crushed it. "What's this Belle Chandler look like?" he asked.

"Fine lookin' big girl," the nighthawk said. "You couldn't hardly fade her for looks. Enough to make a man throw stones at the local girls."

"Black headed?"

"Yeah."

"And a little bigger'n most women in the

places that count?"

"Yes."

"And with smoky-black sort of eyes?"

"That's her, mister. Where'd you meet her?"

"I didn't meet her; I saw her tonight at the hotel dining-room."

"Who was she with?"

"Big shaggy, hard lookin' feller with a mouth like a bear trap and sort of a paunch on him."

"That's Luke, her brother."

Frank drew up a nailkeg and sank down upon it. "What have they done here in Pioche?"

"Bought the Clavenger ranch first, then the Dunlop place, then the Carter ranch. One, two, and three, just like that."

"Well . . .?"

"Mister; those three spreads adjoin one another. The feller who owns all three's got the whole back country beyond Pioche on up Meadow Valley blocked off."

"What of it?"

The nighthawk stiffened. "What of it? Why, damn it all, stranger; my folks and lots of other small cowmen run cattle up along the Muddy north of Pioche for fifty years and made a pretty fair livin' at it. Now

24

– I work in this cussed livery barn because I won't sell my land to Luke and I can't run any cattle over his land to range them up along the river."

"You could sell," said Frank. "What good's a ranch you can't work?"

"I won't sell to Luther Chandler if I starve to death!"

"How about the other small outfits up there?"

"Most of 'em sold to him. Some of the folks refused to sell and packed up an' left. They might as well have sold 'cause he's using their land now anyway. Two others got killed."

Frank's head came up slowly. He said, "Oh . . .?"

"Yeah. One was Evan Morgan, as fine a neighbour as a man could ask for. He refused to move or to sell – and one day there he was, dead in his corral from a slug in the back."

"How about the other feller?"

"Well; I didn't know him too well. He only came in here a year or so back. Young feller though. The word around Pioche was that he was a real good hand with stock an' a sort of quiet, easy-goin' feller."

"He wouldn't sell either?"

The nighthawk frowned. "I don't know, mister. One day some salt-freighters passed his place and there he was – hangin' from the front baulk of his barn twistin' and turnin' in the shadows, shot full of holes."

For a space of seconds Frank was silent. He rummaged again for the tobacco sack and dropped his head to concentrate on what he was doing. "What was his name; you remember that?"

"Harrison. Jess Harrison. He was maybe a year or two older than I was."

Frank lit the cigarette and regarded it steadily. "No," he said. "He was the same age you are."

The nighthawk's head swung. "You knew him?"

"Yes; I knew him. Where was his place?"

"North out of town about six miles. He had a real nice piece of meadow near the river. That's where he built his adobe. Someone fired the barn after Harrison was buried, but the way he built that adobe couldn't nothin' short of a howitzer make an impression on it." As Frank got slowly upright the nighthawk studied him. "Where'd you know this Harrison feller?"

"Over in Colorado."

"Funny, isn't it – you just ridin' in here

and . . ."

"How about saddling my horse for me?"

The nighthawk got up swiftly. "Sure; which one is it?"

"That chestnut gelding in the fourth stall down on the right side."

"Kind of late isn't it?"

Frank smiled thinly, his upper face and eyes hatbrim-shadowed in blackness. "I like to ride at night. It's a sort of habit of mine."

He went back on to the plankwalk and looked southerly. Pioche was empty; a few horses drowsed at the Cattlemen's Club Saloon hitchrail but everywhere else there was hushed darkness. There was no sign of Will but it didn't matter.

He rode north with the river a lapping, strong-smelling companion off to his left for several miles, then he came to a sign nailed to a post. "Trespassing Beyond This Point Forbidden By Order Of Chandler Land & Cattle Company." He rode on.

When the land began to flatten he could distantly see a big peak standing ghost-like in the moonlight dead ahead; to the right of it lay a diminishing range of lesser saw-teeth which were smaller mountains. There was good graze in this area and obviously the Muddy overflowed its banks here whenever

27

there was rain farther north. Frank smelled cattle but didn't see any until shortly before he rode through a broken gate with a high, overhead peeled-log-stringer. There were willows along the riverbank here and a number of old cows came out of them when they heard the jingle of rein-chains and spurs. Frank rode close enough to make out a Rafter C brand.

Another half-mile and he saw the low, square and dark silhouette of an adobe one-room shack. Here there were more cattle; he didn't see them but the smell was strong. Neither did he see the canvas-topped wagon down by the river and because the wind was blowing out of the east his horse did not scent other horses which were encircled by a rope corral near the chuck wagon.

There had once been a wagon trail up to the adobe and beyond, where black char lay in a ragged square darker against the grass than the night. He swung down before the adobe and stood quietly for a moment before ducking past a doorless opening to enter the shack. Wood rats and porcupines had played havoc with cupboards, gnawing anywhere they had scented salt. There were two windows, one on the west wall towards the river and one on the front wall near the door, facing south. Like eyeless sockets, they had no glass and Frank doubted very much if they had ever had it. Clearly his brother had put up this *jacal*, as the Mexicans called these little one-room adobe squares, quickly and cheaply in order to use what little money he'd had for buying cattle. He picked up a gnawed spur strap. It had once held a silver concho; an imprint showed that. Now it was simply a curled, rotting piece of leather. Frank pocketed it. He moved deeper into the room and scuffed refuse with a boot toe. Nothing he recognised as belonging to his brother. Beyond the adobe his horse whinnied. Probably loose horses out there, Frank thought, his attention caught by the faintest scratchings on a side wall; his brother's name and the date. He stood a long moment gazing at this before turning back towards the door.

"Hold it, mister."

Frank froze, startled into immobility. A lean shadow was blanked against the night in the doorway.

"Who are you? What you doin' here?"

Frank's gaze lifted from the black-shiny pistol to the murky face. "Looking for a place to bed down, first off," he said, "and secondly, for a job."

The gun arced away and dropped into a hip-holster. "Come on outside. I can't hardly see you in there."

Frank pushed past the door and turned, facing the rider. "Who're you?" he asked.

"Bent Rodger; Rafter C *remudero* – horse-herder for Chandler."

"You loose a horse?"

Rodgers shook his head. "Nope; heard yours nicker a while back and come over t'see was it one of our'n got loose."

Frank moved clear of Rodger and looked riverward. He saw the wagon then, and inwardly swore at himself. "Round up?" he asked.

Rodger nodded, studying Frank steadily and, Frank thought, suspiciously. Finally he said, "How come you to be ridin' around after midnight lookin' for a job?"

"I told you, Rodger; I was looking for a place to bed down."

"Well; maybe. What's your name?"

"Frank. Frank Baer."

Rodger pushed back his hat, scratched his neck and grimaced. "You'd better get aboard and slope, Frank. This here is Rafter C land. No trespassin' allowed. If it'd been ol' Martin'd caught you instead of me you'd maybe be walkin' back to wherever you

30

come from. Old Martin's pretty touchy 'bout strangers up in here."

"Who's Martin?"

"Ken Martin. Rafter C foreman."

"Maybe if I went over to the wagon with you and hit him up for a job . . ."

"Mister; you wake ol' Martin up in the middle of the night and you'd think the doggoned sky fell on you." Bent Rodger leaned upon the adobe. "Tell you what; Martin's comin' into Pioche tomorrow with one of the wagons for more flour'n such. You just make it a point to be hangin' around the emporium an' hit him up when he comes in."

"How'll I know him?"

"Big, curly-headed feller; sort of shuffles when he walks. Got a dry way of talking. Anyway, he'll be with a wagon carrying the Rafter C painted on it in red."

"Thanks," Frank said, going to his horse and scooping up the reins. "What'd you say your name was again?"

"Bent Rodger."

"Much obliged, Bent."

Rodger straightened up off the wall as Frank swung across his saddle. "Plumb welcome," he said. "Just don't tell ol' Martin I met you here and let you go. He wouldn't

31

like it."

"I won't. Adios."

"Adios."

On the ride back Frank tried to recall Luther Chandler's face but the image of Belle upon whom he'd concentrated instead of her brother blurred Chandler's features hopelessly. Frank grinned to himself. Belle was far more pleasant to think about anyway. She looked good from any angle and would probably continue to do so until hell froze over and for three days on the ice.

Pioche was as quiet as a tomb when Frank rode up to the livery barn and swung down leading his horse forward. An old man came out of nowhere and grinned up at him. "The lad's gone for a spell. I'm takin' his place," he said. "You been here before?"

"Yes. My horse was in the fourth stall down on the north side."

The old man, still smiling – or smirking – nodded bird-like and continued to regard Frank. "Nice night fer riding," he said. A sharp warning struck through Frank. He bent a hard stare on the old man.

"What d'you mean by that, mister?" he demanded.

The old man's bright and faded eyes, alight with a ferret-like wisdom, grew still.

"Nothing. Nothing at all mister. Only the lad said a feller'd rid out tonight. He also said you'd know that young feller – Harrison – what got hung an' shot up."

"And if I did?"

"Oh nothing," chirped the oldster. "Feller can't hardly he'p who he knows, now, can he?"

Frank considered the thin, lined, and weasel-like features through a moment of silence, and again he swore at himself for talking too much. "No," he said, "a feller can't help who he knows – but he can sure put a stop to loose talk, if he wants to."

The old man's face broke into an eroded, sere and lifeless grin. "You know how old I am, mister?" he demanded. "Eighty-one. 'Course, now folks don't pay me much mind, y'see, but there was a time when I said somethin' folks listened."

"I reckon so," conceded Frank laconically, trying to make up his mind whether the old man was foolish or dangerous.

"I got to be eighty-one by keepin' what went in through my eyes from runnin' out my mouth."

"A right smart idea," Frank said, and started to turn away.

But the old man wasn't finished. "Like I

told Charley. Charley Bemis, the nighthawk here who done slipped out to see a girl for a spell tonight. Like I told him: I don't care who you are or why you rode out after dark. You could be figurin' t'rob the hotel safe or the freight office for all of me." The old man winked and turned away.

Frank watched his horse being led away. He took off his hat and slapped a leg with it. "I'll be damned," he said softly aloud, then replaced his hat with a hard jerk and started through the roadway dust towards the hotel.

The old man and the nighthawk had him typed as some kind of an outlaw. This held his interest all the way up to his room and until he was inside. Then he laughed and closed the door. A white patch in the moonlight caught his eye. It was a note which had been slipped under the door. He retrieved it, went to the window and spread it flat on the sill.

"George got in on the evening stage. I told him what you said about other names for you and me, and about seeing the marshal. He says to meet us both at the same place tomorrow night.

Will."

Chapter Three

FRANK spent his time between the livery stable, The Cattlemen's Club Saloon, and the hotel dining-room and by evening had learned three things. One: The nighthawk and the old man had said nothing about Frank's riding out the night before to the day-man, which meant they could be relied upon at least this far. Two: From talk at the saloon, and also around the livery barn, that Luther Chandler was feared much more than he was respected around Pioche. Three: That Belle Chandler lived in town, not out at the Rafter C ranch headquarters, and also that she took all her meals at the Meadow Valley Hotel's dining-room. He had met her gaze over breakfast and again at mid-day. The last time he was sure there had been curiosity in her eyes.

Late in the afternoon with Pioche sinking swiftly into shadows from its barrier of westerly barrancas, Frank bought several cigars and took a seat on the bench outside the hotel where he lit up and smoked, hat tugged forward, and watched people come and go.

He had not encountered Ken Martin and assumed Chandler's foreman had decided for some reason not to come to town after all. It was just as well; Frank didn't want a rider's job. Not yet anyway.

A short and bearded man came up, sighed loudly and dropped down upon the bench. With scarcely a glance at Frank the stranger said, "In this country they'd work you to death then cuss at you for dying."

Frank flicked a gaze sideways. It was the same man he'd seen driving the top-buggy the evening before. Frank watched him light a pipe and suck on it in bubbling contentment. He said nothing but the older man was primed for conversation.

"Newcomer to Pioche aren't you?"

Frank nodded. "Yes; rode in last night. You the mayor?"

The bearded man flashed a quick smile. "No, I'm the doctor hereabouts." He turned and regarded Frank fully. "You have any aches or pains?"

Frank almost smiled. "No," he answered gravely. "Not even a saddle-sore."

"Fine." The medical man settled back and sighed again. "It's pleasant to be able to talk to someone who isn't going to start telling me about their belly or their back or their innards."

Frank said dryly, "Well, Doctor; I'm not

36

likely to tell you about anything."

The doctor was not shaken in the least. "All the better then, young man, because I hate to listen. I'd much rather talk," he retorted.

That time Frank's large white teeth showed in a slow grin. It was more wolfish than amused, however, and he said, "Are you also the undertaker?"

"I am. You want someone planted?"

"No. How is the undertaking business?"

The doctor puffed a moment building up a big head of smoke, then removed his pipe and fastened Frank with a brittle, grey, all-seeing stare. He did not at once answer the question. "Are you familiar with the study of heredity, young man?" he asked.

Frank shook his head.

"Well; I am. I always have been. For thirty years I've been fascinated by the way Nature marks people."

"What's that got to do with the under-taking business?" Frank asked.

"Quite a little. Now take you, for instance. You have very even features. Almost handsome features, you know, except for what exposure has done to them. I'd say somewhere in your background there was some very good blood."

37

Frank gazed at his cigar. "Thanks," he said dryly.

The doctor tamped and re-lit his pipe. He puffed a moment before resuming. "Now; if your question about the undertaking business was supposed to be subtle – it wasn't. It wasn't subtle at all, young man, because I know why you asked it."

Frank looked squarely at the bearded man. "Oh?" he said.

"Yes. You see heredity marked both of you so that an observant scholar would have noticed the resemblance at once, although your brother was easily ten years younger than you are."

Frank became very still.

The doctor's voice dropped a note. "Instead of trying to get information out of me by subterfuge, why didn't you come right out and ask?"

"Ask what, doctor?"

"How your brother was killed and where he is buried."

"All right. Tell me."

The doctor's eyes grew speculative. "I was right, wasn't I; your name is Harrison?"

"My name is Baer. Frank Baer. But tell me about this brother of mine anyway."

38

The grey-sharp eyes remained steady and the voice dropped still lower; it could not be overheard ten feet away. "Baer-Harrison," a shrug. "All right; I understand that."

"About this brother of mine . . ."

"Yes, he was shot first through the head – from the back. Then he was hung in the doorway of his barn and shot into from the ground."

"You're sure he was dead before they hung him?"

"I'm sure Mr. Baer. Very sure."

"What's your name, Doctor?"

"Ambrose Pierce."

"Who killed him, Doctor Pierce?"

"Mr. Baer; let me give you some advice."

"No thanks. I've lived long enough to know free advice usually isn't worth the breath it takes to speak it."

Doctor Pierce searched Frank's face. "You don't believe that," he intoned finally. "No; you're a rather intelligent man. About thirty-two years old, I'd estimate. Right?"

"Exactly right."

The doctor knocked out his pipe and pocketed it. "This was no accidental meeting. You've guessed that haven't you, Mr. Baer?"

"Yes."

"I've seen you going around town today asking questions. Believe me Mr. Baer I won't be the only one who will have noticed that. Now about that advice . . ."

Frank tossed away the cigar and squinted at the thickening dusk. Will and George would probably be waiting. He started to arise. "Shoot," he said.

"You're convinced I'm going to tell you to ride on while you still can, aren't you?"

"Well," Frank said, getting to his feet, turning and gazing down, "aren't you?"

"No sir. I'm going to tell you to avoid Luther Chandler and concentrate on his sister. Luther will have you killed. Belle collects interesting men like I collect books on heredity. She will be attracted to you, Mr. Baer. You are ruggedly handsome; she likes rugged men."

Frank's brows drew down in faint perplexity. "Doctor; I don't understand you but I hope you're not working for Chandler."

Pierce got up. His head came only to Frank's shoulder. "Yes," he said with sudden bitterness, "I work for him. I work for Luther Chandler both as a doctor and an undertaker and I have been working for him in those capacities for two years. He has

Meadow Valley terrified of him and I can show you ten reasons why, north of town across the river at the cemetery. Your brother, I'm convinced, is one of those reasons. I despise that man, Mr. Baer."

Frank said, "Good evening, Doctor. I think we'll see each other again."

He was walking away and did not hear Doctor Pierce say, "I'm sure of it, young man. Absolutely certain of it."

The night was awash with stars and Pioche stood out beneath the cobalt vault of heaven solidly square and functional. Frank passed a saddleshop, a bank, a freight office and several little cafes before he came to the tarpaper shacks again. Beyond them he angled westerly towards the river, went down the footpath and stopped when two hulking shadows arose as though from the ground to bar his way.

Will Harrison said, "What'd you do – crawl all the way?"

Frank ignored him and thrust a strong hand forward. "George; you're looking fit as a six-gun and twice as shiny."

An older man moved into moonlight near the deadfall cottonwood and gripped Frank's hand. He did not at once speak. There was obviously something large in his throat. He was grey, thick in the middle, and attired in a city man's suit.

"Frank, you scrawny old devil," he said finally, pumping his arm vigorously. "It's good to see you. Both of you." He stepped back and starshine shown off a massive jaw and a strong but amiable mouth. What the pale light failed to also show was the identical greeny eyes which Frank also had.

They went to the log and sat down. For a moment there was silence when Frank told about their brother's ranch; what he had learned of Chandler – and finally, in a puzzled tone, of the meeting with Doctor Pierce which had delayed him. As he finished Will Harrison plucked a blade of cured grass and chewed thoughtfully, looking at the elder brother expectantly.

"Tell him what you know," he said to George Harrison.

The older man looked reprovingly at Will. "I don't *know* it," he replied with emphasis, "I only suspect it."

Will shrugged and gazed past at the river. Frank was watching them both. George started speaking. "The marshal's name is Cal Given. I think he's Chandler's man. The reason I think this, Frank, is because when I asked if he had any idea who had killed

Jess he said he didn't have; then he told me that a *smart man* – those were his words – would just pay his respects at graveside and go on back where he came from."

"A warning, George?"

"Yes. I took it to be either a warning or a threat. Given was pretty short with me. He said Pioche had a banker and didn't need another one. He also said Jess was dead and nothing was going to bring him back."

"I see."

Will spat out the blade of grass. "Tell him the rest of it, George," he growled.

"I'm going to. Frank; Marshal Given suggested that I sell Jess's ranch to Luther Chandler."

Frank stood up. "I reckon there's no sense in looking any farther for his killer, is there?" he asked the others.

Will also stood. "No. I'll take care of this Luther Chandler in the morning."

Frank shook his head. "It won't be that easy," he told the younger man. "I ran into Chandler's Rafter C roundup crew out at Jess's place. I think he's got some pretty tough men working for him."

"What of it?"

"Use your head, Will. You kill Chandler and you won't get half way to your horse

43

before they'll kill you."

George Harrison was nodding his head. "That's right. What've you got in mind, Frank?"

"I'm not sure, but I doubt very much if Chandler did the actual killing. Sure; he probably ordered it done, but the man I want is the feller who shot Jess from behind – then Chandler – in that order."

Frank was thoughtfully silent for a long time. George Harrison, watching his face, thought he saw the growing and forming of an idea. "What is it?" he asked.

"This Luke Chandler's made some enemies here in Pioche. He's blocked off part of the upper Meadow Valley range. I wonder if we shouldn't break his back while we're at it."

"How?"

Frank's gaze cleared. "I'm not sure. Give me a day to think about it. We'll meet down here tomorrow night. All right?"

Will would have protested but George cut him off. "Another day or two isn't going to matter. Sure; we'll string along, Frank."

They left the river one at a time and with long intervals between each departure, Frank first, then George, and lastly, Will. There was enough pedestrian traffic on the plankwalks to absorb them should any suspicious eyes be watching and Frank was heading towards The Cattlemen's Club Saloon working his way through the sidewalk traffic when he glanced over his shoulder – and bumped solidly into a body nearly as hard as his own. It stopped him in full stride. He looked quickly forward and then threw out an arm to steady the smoky-eyed woman who was staggering under the impact. "Lady," he said, recognition coming swiftly, "I'm sorry. I wasn't watching."

She put up a hand and fire-points shot from her eyes. They died almost as quickly. "I – guess you weren't," she said. The oddly black-grey eyes studied Frank with open interest exactly as they had done at other times at the hotel dining-room. His hand on her arm tightened perceptibly. She looked at it then back into his face. "I'm all right now," she said, dropping her hand and waiting for him to do likewise. Frank took a step forward, turned with her and began guiding her along without relinquishing his hold.

"I'll see you home, ma'am," he said, softly.

She turned a speculative gaze on him and

opened her lips to speak; evidently decided against it and fell into step soft-pacing the night with Frank's hand supporting her.

They passed nearly half the length of the first square south of The Cattlemen's Club Saloon, then Belle turned down a dusty byway. "That little white house," she murmured. Frank, thinking along with the part he wished to play, said, "I guess I'd best leave you then, ma'am. Your husband wouldn't like it – me bringing you home."

She stopped and looked upwards. "My husband? Oh; you mean the man who was with me at the dining-room?" Her lips curved in a rich smile. "That's my brother. I'm not married, Mr. . . . ?"

"Baer, ma'am. Frank Baer." He returned the smile and continued forward beside her conscious of her fragrance; of their touching arms and thighs and of her long-pacing stride. Thirty lonely-long days on the trail made him terribly aware of the deprivations he had endured without being particularly conscious of them until this moment.

She turned in through a picket gate and started along the board walkway towards the porch. Beyond, the house shone with a ghostly whiteness. He went with her as far as the porch. There, she turned fully towards him, rummaging his features for something.

"Could I fix you some coffee, Mr. Baer?"

"I just finished the biggest supper of my lifetime," he said with a small smile. "But thanks anyway."

"Would you care to sit down a moment, then?" she asked, and when he made no move to comply she faced him again.

"Ma'am; you haven't told me your name."

"Belle Chandler. Now will you sit down?" She was laughing at him and he knew it. He went forward, sat, and removed his hat watching her go to another chair and sit down.

"Are you looking for work Mr. Baer?"

"Not exactly. Maybe later. Right now I'm just sort of looking the country over."

Her amused look lingered. "Do you have to approve of a country before you'll work in it?"

"No," he smiled, "but I always look at a country as though I might settle down in it. I've always done that."

"Do you like what you've seen so far?" she asked with obvious meaning, looking fully into the depths of his eyes.

Frank arose, dumped the hat on the back

of his head and chuckled down at her. "Very much, Miss Chandler. I'd have to be a different man than I am now not to like it – so far."

She also arose. His width of shoulders hid her completely from the roadway. He was looking fully down at her mouth; at its rich outward curvings and its centre fullness. An electric quality came on to the porch with them. She raised her face; the smile was no longer there. "Mr. Baer," she said evenly, "I think you are a reckless man."

He did not smile and their eyes duelled. In a tone that matched hers with unfluctuating evenness, he said: "Belle; unless I'm very wrong you could match me in recklessness or anything else."

Her dark eyes remained unwavering but her lips seemed to thin out a little, to draw back not in challenge but in restraint. On an impulse Frank reached out, caught her gently and drew her slightly forward. Her eyes widened suddenly and grew darker; Frank saw in their depths a sudden want. Their shadows blended, swayed, and clung. His lips found her mouth with strong pressure and she felt the hot hard drive of him; the longing and hunger; the flashing run of his temper. When he released her she hung against him the dull thunder of his slogging heart echoing solidly in her mind. Then she stepped back with a veiled look and parted lips.

"You've been alone too much, Frank," said she almost hoarsely.

"That doesn't matter."

"Yes it does. You haven't been around women lately."

His lips drew back in a cold smile which lacked mirth. "Afraid, Belle?"

"No, not afraid," she said with a quick head-shake. "Satisfied with my life the way it is. I'm not sure I'd want to meet you on your terms. I . . ."

He spun abruptly away and started back down the walk.

"Frank!"

"Yes."

"Give me some time."

He gazed steadily at her with starshine mantling the hardness of his face, softening its angles and square. He did not offer to speak.

"Until tomorrow night at least."

He nodded slightly. "Here, at your house?"

"Yes. At nine o'clock."

He continued on his way, passed through

the picket gate without looking back and strode purposefully back towards the centre of town.

Chapter Four

WILL had been playing blackjack at The Cattlemen's Club Saloon for over an hour when Frank walked in. The full, bold sweep of his brother's gaze touched Will's face only briefly then Frank went past, bound for the bar.

"Ale," he said to the barman and turned, back against the wood, looking out over the room. Town Marshal Given was across the room conversing with a curly-headed large man who was frowning downward as he listened. Nearer, gazing intently at Frank with his grey, all-seeing stare, was Ambrose Pierce.

Smoke hung high in the room and men's voices were blurred in ceaseless continuity. There were some townsmen conspicuous in derby hats among the patrons but generally the Club's clientele was rangemen; riders, freighters, drifters. At the table where Will sat the players lounged freely, hats back and legs out-thrust.

Frank's ale came. He lifted it in a mocking gesture towards Doctor Pierce and drank it off. The medical man looked quickly away, a faintly acid expression on his face.

Frank was restless. He considered buying into the card game but decided against it. He also thought of going to his room at the hotel but that did not fit his mood either. He got a re-fill and went to an empty table and sat loose in the chair thinking of Belle Chandler. But he could not sit like that either; there was too much in him; it had to come out some way. In a ripping curse, a strong drink, a fight or another kiss. A half hour later he went out on to the plankwalk in front of the saloon and paused in the darkness to mould a cigarette. He was lighting it when a swift-low voice spoke out of the shadows behind him.

"Forget *what* she is, Mr. Baer. Remember *who* she is."

"I'm not likely to forget either what or who she is," Frank answered dryly without turning. He recognised the doctor's voice.

"I saw you two on her porch."

"Did you?"

"I set a little boy's broken arm across the road. I saw both of you when I was walking back uptown."

"You've got a way of being in the wrong places, haven't you?"

Doctor Pierce ignored it. "I was at the dining-room this evening, too, Mr. Baer."

"Well; what of it?"

"Did you notice Marshal Given talking to a curly-headed man in the saloon a while back?"

"I did."

"That was Chandler's range-boss, Ken Martin. He and the marshal had supper with Luke Chandler tonight. They sat at a table next to mine. Given told Chandler and Martin about a man named George Harrison coming to town and asking about the killing of his brother, Jess."

Frank's gaze dropped to the dusty roadway and held there. "Go on," he said.

"Chandler told Given to run this Harrison out of town by tomorrow night if he has not decided to leave Pioche by himself before that time."

"Run him out of town – how?"

"Cal Given doesn't need a method or a reason, Mr. Baer. He does exactly as Luther Chandler tells him."

52

Frank said nothing and after a moment soft-padding footfalls faded into the darkness behind him. He turned; Doctor Pierce was scarcely discernible in the blackness.

Frank smoked thoughtfully, flicked away the cigarette and went as far as a dog-trot between the saloon and another building, leaned there with black-night obscurity engulfing him, and waited.

Marshal Given did not leave the saloon until well after midnight. He was walking northward when a blur of movement caught at the corner of his eye and he swung. The fist caught him grazingly along the jaw. Given's knees sagged. An iron grip had him by the shirt-front. It pulled him into the dog-trot and through a fogginess he heard a man growl: "If you touch George Harrison you'll be dead *before* tomorrow night." The second sledging blow crumpled Cal Given in the dust.

Frank was reading the *Carson City Clarion* in the hotel's parlour when Marshal Given came in heading straight for the night clerk. "Ed," he said, "when Mr. Chandler comes in tomorrow tell him to see me at once."

The night-man said "Yes sir," and watched Given stalk back out into the night.

Frank carefully folded the newspaper, laid it aside and went up to his room. He was grinning.

The next morning there was a sifting of dirty clouds overhead and a metallic taste to the air. Rain, Frank thought, riding southerly down Meadow Valley. So it *did* rain in Nevada in the fall. He smiled to himself and hesitated, studying the sky. It had been his intention to find a westerly trail leading up out of the valley so that he could ride northerly along the rims as far north as Chandler's range. Clearly though, he would never make it before those juncturing clouds came together. He shrugged and turned back towards Pioche. Perhaps it was just as well; the ride would have been a long one and he didn't want to be late at the rendezvous with George and Will this night. He had an idea to discuss with them.

Later in the day he bathed and changed his clothes and by supper time was anxious to meet his brothers. He went early, as soon as darkness would mask his movements, to the meeting place. There, however, he had to whittle away half an hour before the others showed up. He spent no time in preliminaries.

"George; Chandler ordered Town

Marshal Given to run you out of town by tonight."

The banker smoked a cigar. This bit of information caused it to jut challengingly. "He hasn't come near me today, Frank."

"No, and I don't think he will." Frank told them of his warning to Given and of how he had roughed up the marshal.

"That'll tip our hand," Will protested.

But Frank wagged his head. "No; all it'll do is make Chandler aware that George isn't alone. Another thing – Chandler's going to wonder which of his cronies, Martin or Given, tipped his hand to whoever is with George. He's going to think it was Martin, I believe. Given wouldn't bust himself in the jaw."

"Well . . ." Will said promptingly. "Now what?"

"I think Chandler's going to pull in his horns a little. He's going to wonder how many of us are with George. He's going to start nosing around trying to find out what we're up to."

George removed the cigar and considered its ash. "Frank; you said that doctor knew who you were."

Following his brother's thoughts Frank nodded. "That's right. I don't think he'll

55

tip our hand but we're not going to take the chance, either. Tonight I've got a date with Chandler's sister." He saw Will's gaze widen and ignored it. "I'm going to work up a meeting with Chandler for tomorrow night if I can."

George continued to regard the ash at his fingertips. "We should be handy," he said. "Chandler never goes anywhere alone. I've watched him enough to know that."

"I'll want Will handy," Frank said, "but not you. You're going to have a belly-ache, George. The clerk at the hotel will send for the doctor for you. You're going to get the doctor to have Chandler's foreman, a feller named Ken Martin, come to your room. After that it's up to you."

"I don't follow you," the banker said, flinging his cigar into the river. "What do I want to see Chandler's foreman for?"

"Offer to sell him Jess's place; use anything that comes to mind, but keep him in your room for as long as you can. After what happened to Given last night Chandler's going to be wondering who is tipping his hand. I want him to think it's his range-boss."

George's face brightened. "I understand. You're using the old axiom 'Divide and

56

Conquer'."

"Something like that," conceded Frank. "Only we're going to feel our way along. I don't know how many of Chandler's crew will fight for him and I don't want to find out. They tell me he's got about twenty pretty handy boys working for him. Those would be pretty big odds."

Will, who had been sitting in thoughtful silence, now said, "Frank; why don't we just cut him down? It could be done pretty easy now that you and his sister are in double harness."

"Will," Frank said irritably, "I told you last night. Chandler probably gave the orders to have Jess killed. We want the man who actually shot him – not just Chandler."

"But he needs killing too," Will exclaimed.

George interrupted. "Let's try it Frank's way," he said to the youngest brother. "Killing Chandler would only drive whoever shot Jess into hiding."

Will considered this and found it reasonable. "All right," he conceded. "What do I do tonight, Frank?"

"Play some blackjack and keep your ears open. Tomorrow night you wait until after dark then get as close as you can to Belle

Chandler's place. There is a cottonwood tree on the east side of the house. Hide in its shadow. If anything goes wrong come a-running." Frank removed his hat, ran bent fingers through his hair and tugged the hat forward again. "We won't be able to meet tomorrow night."

"The following night then," George said, and began moving off.

"The following night if it works out," agreed Frank. "Otherwise the next night."

They left the river separately as before, blending into the darkness, each making his way to a different part of town. Frank, the last one to go forward, veered off into a side street south of the livery stable and approached Belle Chandler's house head-on. A horseman riding slowly past bent a long stare at him and reined down. Frank looked up; it was Town Marshal Cal Given. "Mister," Given said softly, "where you going?"

Frank balanced his answer but decided for the moment anyway to be tractable. "To that white house yonder," he answered, "why?"

Given continued to stare at him. After a moment he said, "I just came from there; she's expecting you."

Frank started forward and the Marshal's

voice hit him in the back.

"What's your name, stranger?"

"Frank Baer."

Given's weathered face became intent and hard. "Baer; you're runnin' on a loose rein."

Frank's brows drew down. "What d'you mean?" he demanded.

The Marshal twisted slightly in the saddle and nodded towards Belle Chandler's house. His meaning was plain enough. "Stay away from that house and the woman who lives in it."

Frank made no answer and after a second hard look Cal Given rode on. Ahead, in the night, a door opened, lamplight spilled out across the porch and Frank saw Belle Chandler standing framed in the opening. He continued forward but slower than before, his mind busy. Perhaps he had chosen the wrong wedge to drive between Chandler and his cohorts; of course he had not suspected that Given was enamoured of Chandler's sister when he made his plans, but now he knew . . . He let the revelation lie dormant, though, as he turned in through Belle Chandler's picket gate.

Yellow light streamed over the blackness of her hair, it limned the vital angles of her figure as she watched him come forward to the porch's edge. She waited for him to speak without smiling, without parting the heavy fullness of her lips. She appeared thoughtful and solemn, and, he thought, she also appeared speculative. He moved up on to the porch seeking her eyes which were shadowed to him. The only movement was a heavy, even rising and falling of her breasts. He felt within himself the urgency of touching her; his eyes closed down upon her losing sight of everything else. Only one part of him remained unaffected; in a small corner of his brain a tiny echo repeated Doctor Pierce's words: "Forget *what* she is; remember *who* she is."

She said in a murmuring low tone, "You met the Marshal." It was not a question. He nodded, silent still. "And he warned you to stay away from me." Another nod.

She looked outward, up the roadway towards Pioche's heart as though Given might still be visible. He wasn't. "Did he frighten you?" she asked.

"No; should I have been frightened?"

Her eyes found his face and he thought her spirit had hardened; had some way turned against him. When next she spoke he understood that her stiffening had to do with Calvin Given, not Frank Harrison.

"Not unless you think that perhaps the game is not worth the risk, Frank."

He relaxed. "I guess you know we're pretty well outlined standing like this," he said.

She too lost her stiffness and turned, leading the way indoors.

The parlour was immaculate, as he had known it would be, and the furniture was good. Seeing his approval Belle moved towards a large sofa. She turned, sat down, and looked up at him on the edge smiling. "We're alone," she said. "You can put your hat down."

He faced her; saw the even darkness of her eyes glowing with something that came from deep within; something tawny and emotionally wind-whipped. He tossed his hat on a table and went to stand in front of her gazing fully and boldly down.

"What we talked about last night," he demanded. "Have you made up your mind?"

"You're very blunt, Frank. Sit down." He sat. She twisted to face him. "You rode out today. Did you like the country?"

"I liked as much of it as I saw. It looked like rain so I came back."

Inside him a warning ran out along his nerve-ends. It was possible that she had seen him ride out, and of course it could have been a natural observation. But then again it might have gone deeper than that. He was grateful now that he hadn't circled around behind Chandler ranch.

"Tell me about yourself, Frank."

The warning became more acute. Her smoky eyes remained strongly on his face. "There's very little to tell," he replied. "I've been a cowboy, a freighter, a wild-horse trapper. Nothing very interesting."

"In Colorado?"

"Among other places, yes," he said, thinking this was too much of a coincidence. She knew something or she suspected something.

"Are you married, Frank?"

He blinked at her. "Of course not; would I be sitting here if I was?"

Her lips parted in an upward curve at his reaction. She almost smiled. "Some men would be sitting here," she murmured. "I made some coffee and little cakes. Shall I get them now or later?"

"Later would suit me," he said, and would have said more but she, seeing the brightening of his gaze, broke in.

"Do you like my home, Frank?"

He settled back with a nod. "I like it fine. You have good taste, Belle. After a few years in cow camps, bunk houses and such, a man forgets things like this."

"I'll get the coffee." She stood up.

Frank came up beside her. She stopped and turned. For the first time he saw her uncertain; unsure of what she should do. He seized that moment and took the initiative. It was not a time for talk though. He reached out, took her by the hips and drew her close to him. She did not resist; there was something confused, sharply bitter-sweet in her expression. He sought her mouth and after a moment his own fire was met and matched by an equal fire. She bruised his lips and clutched his upper arms, then she melted against him and lay there after he'd lifted his face, with the shattered sounds of her breathing in the stillness.

"Frank?"

"Yes?"

"That was easy for you wasn't it?"

He stepped back and looked into her face. "No, it wasn't easy for me, Belle. Of course I wanted to do it – but . . . ."

"But . . .?"

"Nothing. Shall I help you get the coffee?"

"No thanks."

He watched her leave the room; pass through a tasselled opening and fade from sight. He sat back down, twisted up a cigarette and lit it. This, he thought grimly, was no way to fight; this kissing a lovely woman so you can get a shot at her brother. The cigarette did not taste good. He punched it out. When she returned with a tray his mood had changed entirely. They talked after eating and she, perplexed by the change, seemed once more to lose her confidence.

Finally, when he picked up his hat and crossed to the door, Frank said, "Belle; thanks for the evening. It was fine." He continued to gaze at her. "I'd like to see you again – but I've got to find work around here somewhere and that'll probably keep me away for a while."

"No it won't," she said quickly. "I've spoken to my brother. He'll put you on at the Rafter C."

"That's fine," replied Frank with no enthusiasm. "Does he ever come here, to your house?"

"Almost every day; why?"

"Well; would he be coming here, say, tomorrow evening?"

Her eyes smiled. "Yes – tomorrow evening, Frank."

He kissed her lightly; she stood with her hands upon his chest without pressure; then he left and Belle leaned with her back against the door for a long time after his footfalls had faded, feeling the coolness of night against her face and the slowly subsiding tumult within her bosom.

Chapter Five

THE day after his last meeting with Belle Chandler, Frank Harrison rode to the west rim above Meadow Valley and skirted it for six miles to the north. The rain clouds had dissipated the night before without leaving a single drop of moisture anywhere in the area. They had also brought a sultry warmth back to the countryside. By the time he and his mount began the descent into Meadow Valley's northernmost terminus, miles beyond Chandler range, both were perspiring freely.

Here, where the land tilted slightly, Frank had a good view of Chandler's range on both sides of the river. He stopped where a large spring broke out of some trees and rocks to bend its way riverward. The water was cold. There was shade in this spot too, and a layer of leaf mould fetlock-deep to his horse. He smoked looking far out over the Rafter C wondering how much of this Luther Chandler had bought and how much he had taken by force.

The upper valley was broad, grass-matted and sultry. Cattle in groups showed dark red against the lighter colours. Off to the east was a large set of buildings, hull-down on the horizon. That would be Luke Chandler's headquarters ranch. Seeing how remote it was Frank understood Belle's preference for Pioche.

He could trace out his dead brother's place by following broken fences. It looked as though Jess had owned the best meadow land adjacent to the river. Easterly and even southerly for a short ways were the abandoned ruins of other small ranches. These would be the places the livery barn night-hawk had spoken of; no doubt one of them was his.

Chandler had planned well. Across

Meadow Valley at this northernmost terminus the valley was squared-in by upthrust-
ing barrancas on both sides. The farther
south a man owned land, blocking off access
to the upper environs, the greater was his
back-country range.

Frank ground out the cigarette and leaned
back. He was fully relaxed appearing except
for his eyes, but that was an illusion. When
he had first heard of Jess's murder back in
Colorado, his initial impulse had been wild
anger. But after the first few weeks on the
trail to Nevada this had turned to a fixed
and patient purpose. That was what was in
him now; patience; a need for more than
revenge.

In mid-afternoon he stepped across the
saddle and started back the way he had
come. He had seen enough of Chandler
ranch to be familiar with its location, and he
had also seen how his murdered brother's
land lay fist-like and square in the midst of
Luther Chandler's holdings.

The sun was tilting away towards the west
as he retraced his way along the overhead
rim. To the south, running in a long, broad
flow as of an ocean frozen in motion,
stretched Meadow Valley, green against the
dead-grey desert. From that height too, the

Muddy River looked almost inviting the way it shimmered in dancing sunlight.

He was well past Rafter C land when he saw a rider coming along the rim trail from the south. As had happened many times before, Frank's interest and caution came up in about equal parts. He knew the horseman had also seen him; on this plateau there was nothing big enough to hide a man on foot let alone a mounted man; no sage, no trees, no boulders. He reined down to a slow walk studying the oncoming person, who obviously had slowed his own mount for the same reason. When they were less than a quarter mile apart Frank recognised the open, boyish face of Chandler's horse wrangler, Bent Rodger. He halted, waiting for the younger man to come up.

Rodger came on flat-footedly, reins swinging, his head up and his eyes unwaveringly bright in an impassive face. "Howdy," he said, when he halted. "This time you're sort of skirtin' trouble, eh?"

"Staying above it," Frank replied, smiling lazily. "Rafter C doesn't come up here too, does it?"

Rodger shook his head and continued to study Frank. "I guess you never saw Martin, did you?"

"Nope; he didn't show up in town like you said he would."

"He got called back to the ranch," Rodger said, easing his weight over into one stirrup. "You still want the job? Because if you do now'd be a real good time to hit him up. One of the boys quit yesterday right in the middle of the tally and Ken was mad enough to chew nails and spit rust." Rodger's eyes stayed fully on Frank.

"I'll see him," Frank said, "when he comes to town or when I run out of money."

"Yeah," Rodger drawled. "Meanwhile you're sort of gettin' the lay of the land – that it?"

"That's it."

Rodger squared up in the saddle and shortened his reins. "If you get caught down there, mister, like I told you – you're likely to wind up in pretty bad shape." The cowboy pointed with an upflung arm at Frank's tracks leading up from the far downward slope. "After you hire out to Rafter C you'll have lots of chances to know the range."

Frank watched the impassive face; he listened to Rodger's words and weighed the voice and was certain that Rodger was suspicious of him. He said, "I don't see much difference whether I get to know it now or later."

"Them's the rules," Rodger said, and rode on.

Frank watched him for a while noticing how the cowboy went along following Frank's backward trail with his head down. He thought it very probable that Rodger would speak of his obvious suspicions to someone at the home ranch.

He rode back to Pioche and left his horse at the livery barn. As he was leaving a nasal voice spoke from a depth of growing shadows off to one side. "The Marshal was in here askin' about you."

Frank turned and squinted. It was the weasel-wise old man. He was grinning in the same clever-stupid fashion as when they had earlier met. Frank drifted closer to him. "What's he lookin' for?"

"He didn't say; only asked when you rode in, what your name was, and who you seen in Pioche."

"He asked you?"

"Nope; asked the kid, Charley Bemis."

"And . . .?"

"The kid couldn't tell him nothing."

"Thanks," Frank said, and started

towards the roadway.

"Wait a minute, mister. I'm goin' to give you a mite of advice."

Frank stopped and turned. "This is the damndest town for givin' free advice I ever saw. What is it?"

"Stay away from Belle Chandler. Marshal Given's got his rope all shook out to snare her."

"I think he's already made his cast and missed, old timer, but thanks anyway."

He went through a smoky and swiftly falling dusk as far as The Cattlemen's Club Saloon and turned in. The place was nearly deserted; it was supper-time for townsmen and too early yet for the riders to come pounding in from the range. He ate an onion sandwich at the free-lunch table then had a glass of ale. The bartender remembered him and with nothing else to do began a conversation.

"Something fishy goin' on around here," he opined. "It keeps gettin' fishier too."

Frank pushed the glass forward for a refill. When it came he said, "Seems like a pretty sleepy town to me."

"That's because you don't know it like I do. Last night someone worked Marshal Given over and today someone took a shot

71

at Luke Chandler."

Frank's eyes flew wide open. "Here, in town?" he asked, thinking instantly of his brother Will.

"Yep. But that's only half of it, mister. About two hours ago a two-gun man come to town. I guess you know what that means."

"Yes. Who sent for him?"

The barman squinted doorward and there was uneasiness in his shifting gaze. "Dunno. That's what I mean. Pioche's gettin' to feel like a powder keg. There's somethin' in the wind. I know cussed well there is."

Frank drained his glass and pushed it away. Behind him the doors quivered inward and strong footfalls came up behind him, hesitated, then went along the bar and stopped. Frank turned slightly and met the hard and hating gaze of Pioche's Town Marshal. "Ale, Fred," the Marshal called, and finally looked away from Frank.

There was a long interval of stillness. The bartender felt it without understanding it. He shot an upward glance at both Frank and the Town Marshal, then went along the backbar to busy himself sluicing off sticky glasses. Frank made a cigarette. From behind his lashes he saw that Given was watching him with a close, surreptitious attention. As Frank lit up, the marshal turned slightly, standing loose.

"They tell me you're from Colorado," he said. Frank smoked in silence studying labels on the backbar shelves. Given's voice sharpened. "If I was you I'd head back for there. I wouldn't waste no time leavin' either."

"Wouldn't you?"

"No, I wouldn't!"

Frank turned. "I might do that," he said, "when I get good and ready."

Marshal Given set his glass down; he glared. "You're ready right now, mister. One way or another you're ready, the choice is yours."

"What's that mean, Marshal?"

"You go back voluntarily or you go back in a box. Clear enough?"

Frank considered Given's face. It would make no difference what he said now. Given was watching him with a scowl that would believe nothing. "I'll think about it," he said, concentrating on the Marshal's right hand and arm. "If I'm not around by tomorrow night you'll know I took your advice."

Given seemed to be giving Frank's words

some thought. His lips pulled back and his scowl lingered but the look in his eyes dimmed. Then he said, "All right, mister. Until tomorrow at sundown."

Frank dropped a coin on the bar and left the saloon. The first person he saw beyond the spindle-doors was Chandler's horse wrangler Bent Rodger. With him were two men. One was Ken Martin, the other was a thin-faced straight-in-the-saddle two-gun man. Rodger did not at once see him. The trio rode down the centre of the road then angled in towards The Cattlemen's Club Saloon.

Frank avoided a meeting by stepping into a store. He watched the trio dismount and go into the saloon. Given would of course tell them of his ultimatum; probably too in order to enlist their sympathy and support, he would make up a case against Frank.

"Hello, Frank."

He turned. Belle Chandler's hands were clasped around some packages. She was gazing at him with a faint and familiar small smile; in her eyes he saw a scepticism which had not been there before.

"Hello, Belle," he answered. "Thanks for telling the law I'm from Colorado."

Her steady gaze did not waver and

obviously she wished to retain her scepticism as well but he saw her lips change; soften towards him; then a shadow of an expression crossed her features and she sighed. "Someone took a shot at my brother today."

"So the barkeep told me," he said.

"Frank; what do I know about you?"

"Nothing."

She shifted the bundles. "Do you blame me for wondering?"

"I reckon not; but why goad the Marshal; why didn't you wait until tonight and ask me? If I'd taken a shot at your brother, Belle, I'd have told you."

She patently did not believe that, so her smile came again, only wider this time. "Don't worry about the Marshal."

"I'm not worrying, Belle. I just don't want to fight him."

"It wouldn't be a good idea," she conceded. "Especially now. That two-gun man you were watching through the window . . ."

"Yes?"

"His name is Dan Clarke." Seeing no recognition in his face she said, "He's notorious throughout Nevada and Arizona. My brother hired him to ride with the

Marshal."

"Your brother doesn't waste any time," he said dryly. "Maybe he can use another handy man with a gun, Belle."

Her smile grew faint. "You?"

"Me."

"I thought you were a cowboy?"

"I said I've been a cowboy, Belle. I didn't say I was one now." He started away. "I didn't say I was from Colorado either; I told you I'd *been* there." He looked briefly at her. "Same time tonight?"

"Earlier," she replied, "eight o'clock."

He returned to his room at the hotel, had been there only a short while when a soft rap on the door brought him around. A slip of white paper came under the door. He waited, listening to fading footfalls, then went forward.

It was a note from George stating that it had not been Will who had shot at Luther Chandler, and saying also that Will had overheard Marshal Given talking to Belle Chandler about Frank; warning her that he thought Frank had not only shot at her brother but also was related to Jess Harrison. It closed by stating that George was in room ten.

He burned the note, crossed to the

window and looked out over Pioche. He thought ironically that Given was indeed making a case against him and was slanting it to make Belle suspicious and doubtful of him. The ironic part was that although he knew Given was fabricating the entire thing for his own selfish purpose, it was perilously close to the truth.

Chapter Six

WHEN Frank arrived at Belle's home her brother was already there, and with him was Ken Martin, Marshal Given, and the two-gun man. Frank sensed trouble as soon as Belle met him at the door. Her face was sober and her voice a bare murmur.

"Be careful," she breathed to him. "They're out to find out everything they can about you."

He wondered if Will was where he was supposed to be. It had been too dark as he came up to see him. Belle was introducing them. Frank shook Luther's hand and dropped it. He looked steadily at Cal Given without speaking or nodding. The two-gun man, Dan Clarke, inclined his head stiffly without speaking.

Belle excused herself and passed from sight towards the rear of the house. Marshal Given found a chair and sat in it, his shoulders sloping forward. Luther Chandler, slit-lipped and menacing, continued to stand. Behind him Ken Martin and Dan Clarke seemed the most thoroughly relaxed and the least interested but Frank was not fooled.

"They tell me you're a Coloradan," Chandler said to Frank, and the latter saw instantly at close range that Luther Chandler was a dangerous man; he was dark-eyed like his sister, hard, ruthless and scarred by violence. Frank thought only a bullet would ever stop Chandler if he became aroused.

"I've been in Colorado," Frank stated. "I've also been in Wyoming and Montana – but that doesn't make me from those places."

"That's a cute answer," Given growled. "Just exactly where do you come from, Baer?"

"You're the mouthy one that's been saying I'm from Colorado. If you're sure of that why ask me now where I'm from?"

Given flushed and Luther Chandler, as tall as Frank but much heavier, went to a chair and sat down. His eyes were agate-still with a speculative light moving in their depths.

"Where *are* you from?" he asked.

"Idaho."

"What part?"

"Ash Fork," answered Frank brusquely.

"Never heard of it."

Frank's anger was mounting. "I reckon there are lots of places in Idaho you've never heard of," he retorted. "Now let me ask a question: What's this all about?"

Chandler looked at Given and leaned back. His voice changed and a little of the hardness left his eyes. He said, "Someone took a pot-shot at me as I was ridin' into town today. The Marshal figures it might've been you or some other stranger."

Frank snorted. "If someone took a shot at me I'd know cussed well they weren't any stranger." He swung his head towards Given. "And if I'd done it Chandler wouldn't be sitting here now, either."

The two-gun man's lips drew down approvingly; obviously he had been thinking the same thing.

Marshal Given was uncomfortable. He

79

looked balefully at Frank but avoided Chandler's cool stare. Ken Martin, who until now had stood back in the shadows across the room, walked towards the sofa and sank down there. He too watched Given. After a while he said, "Cal; I know what you're doing, but I think you'd better go about it some other way. We got enough trouble 'thout you throwin' dust in our eyes because you're jealous."

Given was stung; his colour mounted and he sprang up. "Damn you, Ken. For a plugged nickel I'd . . ."

"Sit down," Chandler said. "Sit down, Cal."

Given sat.

Chandler crossed his legs and dropped an appraising gaze on Frank. "My sister tells me you're a handy man with a gun. Is that right?"

"I'm still alive," Frank said succinctly.

Chandler turned this over in his mind. He was on the verge of speaking again when Belle returned with a tray, cups, and coffee. Her brother's lips snapped closed while she set the things on a table and cast a searching look at the men. "There is sugar in the bowl," Belle said, moving back, "help yourselves."

Frank was getting to his feet when a sharp roll of knuckles over the front door echoed into the room. Belle moved forward. None of the men spoke while they got their coffee and stepped back.

"It's for you, Ken," Belle called.

Martin looked up quizzically, then put aside his cup and crossed the room. Chandler, whose back was to the door, stirred his coffee while gazing at Frank. "Belle says you want work," he exclaimed. "Is that right?"

"It was, up until about fifteen minutes ago," Frank answered.

Belle was approaching them when her brother followed his next sentence with a slow-growing scowl. "What d'you mean by that?"

"It's pretty simple," Frank drawled. "I don't like the smell of the lot of you. I don't think I'd work for you, Chandler, if there was no one else hereabouts to work for."

Chandler was turned to stone. Cal Given's expression of solid dislike turned to purest astonishment and the two-gun man's stirring hand grew suddenly still. Belle, standing beside Frank, stared upwards in disbelief; in puzzlement and uncertainty, and these mingling emotions gave her face an odd sweetness. "Frank!" she said.

He ignored her and held Luther Chandler's eyes with their increasing great flare of wrath. "Where I come from folks don't pussyfoot around; when they've got something to say they come right out and say it. If you thought I took that shot at you, why didn't you ask me?"

Chandler continued silent and Cal Given looked from Belle to Frank and over at Chandler. "What kind of tomfool talk is this," he demanded. "I told you, Luke; this feller means trouble." Given was hungering for trouble; it was in his eyes and the shape of his mouth as well.

But Chandler, recovered from his surprise, was looking at Frank in a new way; it might have been with respect and it might just as easily have been with deadliness; Frank did not know. But he did know that he had jarred Luther Chandler away from his suspicions; had jarred him into this mood of thoughtfulness which now held him.

It was Belle who broke the ensuing moment of drawn out silence. She said, "Luke; I think you'd better go now. You and your friends."

Luther Chandler put aside the untouched

coffee, took up his hat and jerked his head doorward. Given and Dan Clarke moved off obediently but Chandler did not at once trail after them. He said to Frank, "Mister; I wonder just how good you really are with that gun."

In a tone of matching softness Frank said, "I know just one way for you to find out, Chandler. Unless you'd rather let Clarke do it for you."

Chandler put his hat on. "You staying at the hotel?"

"I am."

"I'll come up and see you later tonight."

"I'll be waiting."

Chandler shot his sister a look and followed Cal Given out into the darkness closing the door gently behind himself.

Belle blew out a long breath and moved up to face Frank squarely. "I don't care how good you are with that gun," she snapped at him, "you had three-to-one odds against you."

He sipped some coffee and regarded her over the cup's rim. "No, not really, Belle. Your brother wouldn't have let anything start here in your house."

She took him by the arm towards the sofa and sat. "You're not a very good judge of men, Frank. My brother would start a fight anywhere; I know!"

Frank did not disagree with her, but remembering Luther Chandler's eyes he believed himself to be right. He thought with a shrug that the next time they met it might be very different; probably would because very obviously Chandler was not a man who overlooked a slight or forgot an insult.

Evidently Belle was thinking along the same lines because she suddenly said, "What on earth made you say that to Luke – about not working for him if he was the last man in the country to work for?"

"He asked a question and I answered it," retorted Frank. "He wanted the truth and he got it."

"Frank; you must be insane. People don't talk to Luke like that."

A rush of hot irritation passed over his face and he got up. "Thanks for the coffee, Belle." His hat lay where she had put it on a little marble-top table. He got it.

"Frank," she said sharply, her expression smooth and tight and disturbed. When he faced around her tone altered, turned soft again. "You don't have to go."

"I've got a date to meet your brother," he

said. "Remember?"

She swept up close to him with displeasure marring her beauty; displeasure and genuine puzzlement. "I don't understand you. Do you – are you going to *fight* him?"

"That lies with him, Belle, not me."

"Oh Frank; please stay . . . for a while anyway."

He gazed into her face noticing how badly her poise was shattered by perplexity over him. "Not tonight, Belle. Maybe not any night. You're as bad as the rest of them. You've been nosing around too. You've let that clown of a Town Marshal twist you around his finger with his . . ."

"That's not true," she flared out, her anger showing now in the narrowing of her eyes; in their sudden loss of warmth. "Cal Given's a fool; I've told my brother that a dozen times. He's worse than that – he's dangerous."

Frank grunted derisively, goading her. "Given's not dangerous; he's too house-broke by Luther to be dangerous. He's simply a jealous, treacherous fool."

"You don't know!"

"Like hell I don't," he shot at her. "I've known a hundred just like him. I've also

85

known some like Dan Clarke. You think he'd protect your brother if someone offered him an extra thousand dollars to look the other way next time someone takes a pot-shot at Luke? If you do you're as simple as Given is."

Her lips parted, the colour drained from her face as though Frank had struck her and her eyes widened in a hot, black stare.

"Would you offer Clarke the thousand, Frank?"

"Don't be silly; of course not."

"You're a truthful man, aren't you?"

"I told you I wouldn't give Clarke a cent."

"I didn't mean that. I meant – you wouldn't lie to me would you?"

He smashed his hat on and shouldered past her towards the door without speaking. She caught him there, flung herself against him. He thought, seeing her now in the faintest moonlight coming past the opened door, that she was not the same self-assured, poised, almost scorning woman he had seen that first night in Pioche at all, and as though she read his thoughts she drew back from him and her face, pale in starshine, smoothed out.

"You wanted me on your terms, didn't

you?"

He said nothing.

"All right, Frank. On your terms."

He reached upwards with surprising gentleness and traced out the smooth rounded curve of her throat and let his fingers lie still against her flesh. "I think it is too late," he told her. "If it wasn't too late right from the start, Belle."

"What do you mean?"

Instead of replying he moved his hand up under her chin, cupped it there and forced her head back. He kissed her with tenderness, with solemnity, and felt the turmoil dissolve under the pressure of his lips. She moved back suddenly staring at him.

"On any terms you want to impose," she murmured. "Only stay with me, Frank."

He left her framed in the doorway. Walked strongly back uptown unaware that behind him Belle Chandler's face had slowly mottled with shame, with wild anger at offering herself and being scorned. He was equally as unaware of the dark shape which detached itself from the night's formless substance across the roadway and trailed soft-footedly along behind him, or the third, taller shadow which came out of the gloom beside Belle's house and hesitated a moment

87

before moving off behind the first dark shape.

The Cattlemen's Club Saloon was crowded. Frank saw the burdened hitchrail when he turned north on to Pioche's main thoroughfare and started along it. He had thought of having a drink before going to the hotel but now he changed his mind. Some big cow outfit was in town in force; he didn't feel like bucking a crowd right then. He continued on past, cut into a dog-trot between two buildings and came out into a refuse-littered back-lot behind the hotel. Here, he waited a long moment seeking movement, and although he saw nothing suspicious behind the hotel a sound of gently placed footfalls came from behind him in the dog-trot. It at once crossed his mind that he had been followed from Belle Chandler's house. It could be a Rafter C rider, he thought, ordered by Luther to see that he came to the rendezvous. Then he knew differently; the skulking man coming down the dog-trot wore no spurs. Given, he told himself; the jealous Town Marshal.

Frank drew back into the darkest edge of the hotel's shadow and waited. The footfalls came closer, steadily moving but muffled. Then Given emerged into the back-lot and stopped for a long look. Frank swung forward with a looping blow and the Marshal curled downwards into the dust without a sound. His holstered gun slid forward to lie shiny in the darkness.

Frank faded back and waited. There was no movement ahead. He waited fully two minutes then made his cautious way along the back wall to a rear entrance and pushed inside. A lamp was burning feebly from an overhead bracket. By its shifting light Frank made out a stairway. He climbed slowly upwards putting each foot down close to the wall where the boards would not squeak. He flattened at the landing peering down the hallway. There was no one in sight. He then strode boldly forward, entered his room and softly closed the door. No one was waiting for him but obviously someone had been there ahead of him. His saddlebags had been emptied over the bed. He blew out a big breath; that too would have been Given's work. Luther Chandler was smarter than to expect an enemy to ride into his town carrying anything incriminating. He went forward and commenced cleaning up the mess. Afterwards he made a cigarette, sat by the window in darkness, and waited.

Chapter Seven

LUTHER CHANDLER entered Frank's room without knocking shortly before midnight. With him was the two-gun man. Chandler halted, squinting towards a man-shape near the window. "Light the lamp," he said. Frank made no move to comply. He could see them both perfectly despite the gloom.

"I'll light the lamp," he retorted, "when you send Clarke downstairs."

Chandler teetered on his toes evidently seeking the reflection of a naked gun in the shadows. "Clarke stays," he said shortly. "What you afraid of?"

"The odds," Frank answered. "Sit down Chandler. You too Clarke."

Chandler groped his way to the bed and sank down there. Clarke remained back by the door.

"You talk pretty big," Chandler said menacingly. "You made a pretty big noise back at Belle's place, mister. How'd you like to back it up now that we're alone?"

Frank's teeth shone in the darkness. "I figured you'd talk like this, Chandler," he stated. "That's why it's dark in here. I've been waiting in this darkness for a couple of hours. My eyes are used to it, so if you want to play the odds go right ahead."

Chandler held his silence for a moment, then said, "Who are you; what do you want in Pioche?"

"I had a job in mind when I came here," Frank answered. "Now I guess I'll just hang around to see the fun."

"Marshal Given ordered you to leave town, didn't he?"

"I'm still here, Chandler. Where's Given?"

Chandler leaned forward. His breath whip-sawed in the darkness. "You!" he exploded. "You're the one who hit him!"

"Any time he dogs me he's likely to get hit. That goes for anyone else you put up to it."

Over by the door Clarke shifted his weight and the floor squeaked. Chandler shot him a peering look then returned his attention to Frank. "You got him the other time, too, didn't you?"

"I don't know what you're talking about, Chandler."

It sounded believable and Chandler leaned back, more puzzled than ever. After a time he said, "Is that the only reason you hit him; because he was trailing you?"

"That's the only reason."

"How about friends," Chandler asked. "You got any friends among the townsmen or ranchers?"

"Not a one," replied Frank. "I've never been in Pioche before in my life."

Chandler mulled this over a moment, then his entire attitude changed. "Baer, isn't it?" he asked.

Frank said, "That'll do."

"Baer; how'd you like to work for me at better'n rider's pay?"

"I told you what I thought of working for you at your sister's place."

"Listen; forget all that. What the hell, man; you were a stranger an' I'd just been shot at. You've got to make allowances."

"Whether I worked for you or not Given'd still try to get a crack at me."

Chandler got up. "No; not if I tell him not to. How about it? Twice rider's pay and you'll be your own boss."

"Doing what?"

"I need a man right here in Pioche. Cal Given's failed me twice now. I need a man to watch him and to listen to the talk. Someone's out to kill me. I want to get him before he gets me."

"Use Clarke, there."

"Clarke's my bodyguard. Well?"

"I'll let you know." Frank also arose. "I'll ride out to the ranch tomorrow evening if I decide to take your offer."

Chandler's impatience showed in a nettled frown. Then he went towards the door saying "I'll be waiting."

Frank listened to their retreating footfalls and made a cigarette. He smoked it down to the end then went out into the corridor. The hotel was as silent as a tomb. He went to room ten and tried the latch; it was bolted from within; he rapped softly, heard a bed squeak and a moment later looked into the solitary dark eye of a cocked pistol. He pushed it aside and swiftly entered. George was in a voluminous nightgown. He frowned and put the gun aside.

"How'd you make out?"

"All right," the older man replied. "Doctor Ambrose got Martin up here. I tried to sell him Jess's place. He laughed at me, said no one would buy it and that Chandler had the use of it anyway. How about you?"

"Chandler wants me to work for him here in Pioche."

"Well?"

"I don't know; maybe I'll do it. Where's

Will?"

"He's staying at a rider's rooming-house beyond the Marshal's office. Why?"

"Are you positive he didn't take that crack at Chandler?"

"Absolutely."

"How can you be so certain; were you with him?"

"No; but I saw the man who did the shooting."

Frank's eyes sprang open. "Where; who was he?"

"He shot from the livery barn roof. I don't know who he was. A young fellow, about Jess's age, fair-haired, slim. Not the gunman type at all, Frank."

"I'll be damned," Frank exclaimed. "Charley Bemis – the nighthawk at the stable."

George's dry rejoinder was: "I hope he's better with horses than he is with a short-gun. He missed Chandler a mile. Do you know him, Frank?"

"Just to talk to. Chandler froze him out on one of those upriver ranches. I knew he hated Chandler's guts but I never took him for a bushwhacker."

George Harrison yawned then said, "You haven't lived long enough yet, Frank; any man will become a bushwhacker if he broods long enough, even a nice looking young feller like this Bemis."

Frank wasn't listening. "Can you get word to Will?" he asked. George perched on the edge of his bed and nodded. "Then tell him to watch for Chandler tomorrow and if he shows up in town to take a shot at him. A near-miss."

It was George Harrison's turn to look surprised. "Are you serious, Frank?" he demanded. "What for?"

"Because Bemis is going to have another near-miss also. Maybe I'll even join in."

"What's the purpose; to terrify Chandler?"

"Something like that," Frank retorted. "Would it work with you, George?"

The elder Harrison looked wry. "Just one near-miss would be enough for me." He groped for a cigar in a coat pocket, lit it and settled back on the bed fixing Frank with a probing look. "What about the girl?"

"I can't use her, George. It sticks in my craw, getting at Chandler through her."

George nodded and for a moment let his gaze wander, then he said, "What about the Marshal?"

"I knocked him out again tonight.

Chandler said he'd call him off, but I think it's gone too far with Given for that."

"I've heard around town," George said, "that he's got his eye on Chandler's sister. Is that what you mean?"

"Yes."

"Will could take care of him. So far no one's connected him with either of us, I'm sure of that."

Frank crossed to the door. "No; I'll take care of Given. Just get word to Will about taking a wild shot at Chandler."

"I will. Frank; tomorrow night down by the river?"

"Yes. Goodnight, George."

"Goodnight."

The stillness held. When Frank was back in his room he crossed to the window and sought the moon. It was well down the sky and he surmised it to be close to three o'clock in the morning. He stood there feeling the night's sharpness and did not retire for another hour. When he awoke the following morning there was a greyness to the early hours. By the time he got downstairs into the hotel dining-room there was also thunder rolling out of the east. The air hung close and unstirring out in the roadway. This time, he thought, it will

96

surely rain.

Frank Harrison was a stranger to Nevada; he had no idea *how* it rained there.

After breakfast he went to the livery barn. The proprietor was there and while Frank was looking in on his horse the grinning wise-stupid little old man shambled in with a high cackle. "Goin' to rain like a . . ." He saw Frank and let it dwindle off. The liveryman mumbled assent and departed.

"Come here," Frank called. The old man moved deeper within the draughty barn. "Where does Bemis live?"

"Charley? Well sir; you go 'round back o' the hotel and there's a sort of half log, half plank shack there. He moved in there after he come down from the ranch. Why? You want to see him?"

Frank put a hand on the old man's shoulder. "Remember what you told me about why you've lived so long?" he asked, and removed the hand when he went past. "Might be a good thing if you thought about that a little the next time you feel like asking questions."

Outside the wind was beginning to scrabble along under eaves with a sobbing sound. Frank leaned into it as far as Bemis's shack and struck the door hard. It opened inward

97

and a tousled head thrust past. "Dammit; I work nights, mister, and need some sleep."

Frank pushed inside and closed the door. Bemis drew up scowling. He waited for Frank to satisfy himself they were alone and faced him with wind rising beyond the door.

"Too bad you missed yesterday," Frank said. "I'd have thought you'd be a better shot than that."

"What kind of crazy talk is this, anyway," Bemis said in garrulous protest. "Listen, mister . . ."

"You listen, Bemis. You're goin' to take another shot at him today."

"A shot at who? What the hell are you talkin' about?"

Frank ignored Bemis's protests. "And you're going to miss again, too. Remember that; don't hit him. Just kick up some dust beside him." While Bemis stared Frank drew a twenty dollar gold piece from a pocket and put it down in plain sight on a rickety table. "Remember now, Bemis – a near-miss is all I want."

The nighthawk went to the table and stood looking at the coin. "You're after him too, aren't you?"

"Yes. But I don't want him dead. Not yet. So you miss him, hear?"

"I'll miss him. Yesterday I didn't mean to though; my foot slipped on the roof when I shot or he'd be dead now."

"And don't get caught."

Bemis picked up the coin as he turned. "I won't, don't worry about that. Tell me something, mister; what's your interest in Luke Chandler?"

"Remember me telling you how old Jess Harrison was?"

"Yes; you knew him in Colorado. Was he a pardner of yours or something?"

"He was my brother, Bemis. My youngest brother."

"I should've guessed something like that," Bemis said, showing no surprise at all. "But say; have you seen that two-gun man Chandler's hired to protect him?"

"Yes. You watch him like a hawk when you shoot. He's lightning fast they tell me."

Charley Bemis was staring at Frank and wagging his head. "It's not me that's got to watch out, Harrison, it's you. If Luke finds out Jess was your brother you'll be a dead duck."

Frank crossed to the door and nodded without speaking as he passed through.

The sky was very dark now although it was not yet nine o'clock in the morning of a

99

fall day. As long as the wind blew Frank did not think it would rain. When it slacked off and the air became very still, oppressively heavy, the rain would come.

He went to The Cattlemen's Club Saloon and saw the barman's eyes widen at sight of him. He grinned. "I think the Marshal changed his mind. But if he hasn't I have; I kind of like it here in Pioche. I don't think I'll leave after all."

"Ale?" The barman asked in a dead voice.

Frank inclined his head and turned to gaze out the window. Wind-whipped dust was rising cloud-like; shutters rattled and somewhere a piece of metal banged with echoing irregularity. A group of horsemen cantered past heads tucked low and hats pulled down hard, riding in from the north. Frank thought he glimpsed Bent Rodger among them but wasn't sure. Then they were gone and the wind rose to a steady howl.

"Here's your ale, mister."

Frank reached around and took it and the barman retreated to a guttering lamp which he took down with a curse to trim the wick. Except for two old men over against the wall, oblivious to everything but their checker game, Frank and the barman were alone in the saloon. Outside there rose a wind-muffled call, the stamping of spurred feet and six riders burst past the door slapping at their clothing and rubbing their eyes. Bent Rodger was in the forefront. He saw Frank at once and made an almost imperceptible nod in his direction, then led off towards the far end of the bar.

A storekeeper came running in off the plankwalk gasping. To no one in particular he said, "What a storm; hey Fred; give me a quick one. I got to get back."

A solitary figure pushed purposefully past the doorway and stopped to throw a wide glance over the room. It was Ken Martin of Rafter C. His heavily-lashed eyes met Frank's gaze, lingered briefly then went along the bar where Chandler's riders were lounging. Martin angled in that direction.

The wind died away suddenly and Frank saw the first raindrops explode in the roadway kicking up dust. Where they hit the saloon roof it was with the sound of small fists striking. They were as large as spur rowels and gradually increasing. People scurried past out on the plankwalk. The air became still and fragrant. Pioche waited, bracing into the coming storm, the increasing downpour, and finally the water came in sheets; wind-frayed perpendicular sheets which marched one behind the other over the town with a strong roaring.

Marshal Given stamped in out of the storm his shirt rain-darkened and his hat dripping water. He did not at first look in Frank's direction because Ken Martin called his name. Not until he was moving did he see Frank and instantly his face darkened.

Chapter Eight

A STEADY roaring filled Pioche and water turned the roadway into a violent plank-walk-bordered river. Frank's interest was divided between this uncommon storm and the group of men farther down the bar. He turned eventually to face forward so that he could watch the Rafter C men and Marshal Given.

Behind him several newcomers entered the saloon. One of them stamped his feet and laughed. Another man pushed through the spindle-doors and behind him came Frank's tallest brother. Will and three other men called for cards and went directly to a table. In the backbar mirror Frank saw Will's slow gaze run along the bar and back again. Their glances crossed then Will sat down.

Two men left the Rafter C crowd and came steadily along the bar. Frank turned, feeling no surprise that Chandler's foreman and Marshal Given were coming towards him together. He waited for them to stop, which they did facing him. Over their shoulders he saw the cowboys lounging too loosely; as though anticipating something.

With no preliminary Given said, "I told you to leave Pioche by sundown, Baer."

Frank nodded, looking at Martin whom he considered by far the more dangerous of the two. "You did. What of it?"

Given sucked back a breath but Martin cut in. "You should've gone, mister," he said slowly, with weighted words. "Pioche can be pretty unhealthy at times."

Frank considered the rangeman before he replied. "Before you buy into this private feud," he growled, "you'd better talk to Chandler. He wants me to stay in Pioche."

Martin's eyes wavered. "When did he say that?" he challenged.

"Last night. Go ask Dan Clarke if you

doubt me."

Martin turned silent. He shot a look at Given; Frank thought he'd detected suspicion in it. The Marshal's face coloured, which gave Martin his answer. He moved back slightly to lean upon the bar evidently withdrawing from the discussion.

"You hit me last night," Given accused. "And you been snoopin' around up at Rafter C."

Frank's eyes showed scorn. "You asked for it, slippin' up on me in the dark. What'd you expect me to do – wait for a back-shot?"

"You're another brother to Jess Harrison, too."

"If I was," retorted Frank, "would that be a crime?" He hooked a thumb in his shell-belt. "Given; you talk too much. I wonder that Chandler hasn't tumbled to you yet; double-crossing him every chance you get; lying to his sister; lying to his men; blowin' up a big smoke behind that star you wear – and hollow clean through."

Cal Given stepped suddenly away from the bar, his face gone white and his lips compressed into a cruel line. He was going to draw his gun; Frank knew it and took a swift forward step pushing the lawman off balance. He swung from the belt and Given sucked back. The blow grazed upwards knocking Given's hat off but otherwise doing him no injury.

Someone let off a yelp. Frank thought it was Ken Martin and swung sideways to watch Chandler's range-boss. But Martin was still leaning on the bar; he was watching from beneath heavy brows and making no move to interfere. He seemed in fact to be enjoying the fight.

Given tried again to draw his belt-gun. That time Frank rocked him with a blow to the side of the head. Given's arms dropped, he staggered back and twisted sideways with visible effort to escape the next blow. Then he back-pedalled, letting his head clear by trading space for time. Frank did not press him; he was enjoying this; there was a sloshing full heartbeat in his head, a quickening of perception and a looseness to his muscles. He stalked Given, white from throat to hairline except where his eyes burned with some primitive eagerness for battle. Stalked him half across the room and hit him a meaty blow in the belly and hit him again higher, in the chest, and half spun Given around with a third blow. Then he went up close, reached down, removed the lawman's pistol and tossed it backwards on to the floor.

But Frank made a bad mistake. He underestimated Given. He thought he was worse beaten than he was and got too close. Given brought up a whistling strike that connected solidly and Frank nearly fell. His head roared with a louder sound than the storm was making and he had trouble seeing.

Given went forward on the offensive boring in fists flailing, head low and shoulders hunched forward. Frank was rocked several times. He covered up, dropped his head behind a shoulder and pawed outward trying to keep Given off. The Marshal beat past his guard, hurled himself forward with an explosive breath and threw a great upper-cut which missed. He then fell against Frank and burrowed his head in to protect himself. Frank brought up a knee and Given cried out. Frank tried to break free but Given was hanging on desperately; he inched his fingers upwards seeking Frank's face, his eyes. Frank reached out around the lawman, locked his hands and brought to bear his full and considerable strength. Marshal Given squirmed; he fought for breath and he rained blows on

Frank's head. He sawed and whipped trying to break the crushing grip. His breath whooshed out and his mouth stayed wide, sucking for air that could not enter his lungs.

Frank squeezed until the room swayed and brilliant little sparks burst in his vision. Given's blows were diminishing in force; his body was slackening. Frank flung both arms away and stepped back. Given almost collapsed; he swayed there, helpless, and Frank struck him twice more, once in the middle and the last time solidly along the jaw. Marshal Given went down; he slid forward on the plank flooring and did not move again. The room was without movement and except for the roaring downpour overhead and outside, there was not a sound.

Frank looked at the other men solemnly watching him from the bar and over at Will's table. Most of them were gazing at Cal Given. Ken Martin turned bar-ward with deliberate slowness and called for a drink. When the barman came up to comply the spell of silence and stillness was broken. The Rafter C men spoke quietly among themselves, a few returning to their drinks. At Will's table the men, close-faced against any idea that they might interfere, took up their cards with elaborate unconcern. Beyond, in the millrace roadway a gunshot slammed without echo into the rainfall's constant thunder. Martin flung around. His men also turned, instantly alert. A second shot sounded, deeper, more throaty this time which meant it was a short-gun not a rifle or carbine, and everyone rushed past Frank towards the door and windows. Will too, swept past still holding his cards. He husked to Frank as he went by: "That was George. I'll explain later."

Instead of following the others out on to the plankwalk, Frank stepped over Cal Given, went to the bar and leaned there. Without a word passing between them the bartender brought up a bottle, an empty glass, and moments later a second glass filled with water. Frank drank, ignored the water and pushed his shirt-tail back into his trousers. Behind him men were calling, their shouts quivering briefly in the storm. He turned to look road-ward and behind him the barman said very quietly, "You made a bad mistake, mister. You should've baited him into drawing."

When Frank looked around the barman was moving off obviously wishing to pursue this conversation no further.

Ken Martin was the first man to re-enter the saloon. He studied Given's limp form a moment then pushed on past to halt beside Frank. "I never liked for a man to use me," he said. "I said yesterday for him to quit throwin' dust in everyone's eyes 'cause he was jealous of you hanging around Belle."

"You're not the only one he's used," Frank replied. "He lied to Belle about me and said I took that shot at Chandler."

Martin began wagging his head. "After we left Belle's place I told Luke you didn't do that. You see, Bent Rodger told me about seein' you up on the rims about the time Luke was bein' shot at." Martin's heavily-lashed eyes were wide with wonderment. "You got more witnesses now than you had then, too."

"What do you mean?"

Martin jerked his head sideways towards the roadway. "A couple more shots fired at Luke just now out there in the rain."

Frank knew Martin was watching him closely; he made a slightly surprised expression come up around his eyes. "Is that what the shooting was, out there; another bushwhacking attemp at Chandler?"

Martin nodded, studying Frank. "You

couldn't have done it this time either." Martin flagged the barman. Out of the corner of his mouth he said, "Want another drink?"

Frank leaned forward. They shared a drink and Martin looked steadily into the backbar mirror. "He'll be along directly, Baer. When Luke's roiled up it pays to just listen."

The Rafter C riders hauled Marshal Given to a chair and propped him into it. He groaned and one of them held his head back while another one grinningly poured a jolt of whisky down him. Given coughed and threw up his arms. The cowboys laughed. Frank and Ken Martin turned to watch. At that moment Luther Chandler and his two-gun shadow stalked into the saloon. Chandler's face was pale and his eyes shone dangerously. He was wet even beneath his slicker and caked mud lay heavily on both his feet. For a moment he glared at his foreman and Frank standing together at the bar then he saw Cal Given hanging loosely in the chair opening and closing his mouth and crossed to where the lawman sat to stand over Given huge and menacing. The cowboys discreetly withdrew to the bar adding to the sudden silence by their stillness.

Chandler turned abruptly away from Given. "What happened here?" he demanded of Ken Martin.

"A fight," the range-boss said laconically. "Him and Baer. Cal came off second best."

"A fight about what?"

Martin's answer was brief. "Cal called him, Baer lit into him – and there's Cal."

The black-grey eyes switched glitteringly to Frank. They found their match in the greeny cold stare that did not fail before them. Chandler seemed suddenly to be listening to a small voice; he turned finally, tore the marshal's star from Given's shirt, crossed over and flung it down on the bar in front of Frank. "Put it on," he said sharply. "From now you're working for me as Pioche's Town Marshal."

Frank looked down at the star and up into Ken Martin's face. He thought there was a hint of a cold smile around the foreman's mouth. Farther along the bar half a dozen bronzed faces were watching him. He deliberately reached over the lawman's nickel circlet, got his drink and finished it, his back to Luther Chandler. "What's the pay?" he quietly asked.

"Twice what Given got."

"Put it in dollars."

Chandler was reddening; no one ever spoke to him with their back turned. He saw his foreman turn and gaze at him. "Two hundred dollars a month. Now put on that badge."

Frank pinned the circlet to his shirt and looked at it as he faced Chandler. "The first month in advance," he said. "I've got a feeling this might not be a real healthy job."

Someone laughed at the card table. Chandler spun around. All the men at Will's table were suddenly engrossed with their game.

Chandler fished out a roll of bills, peeled several off and threw them down. Then he said, "Find out who that was shot at me. There was two of 'em." He glared at Dan Clarke. "*He* never even saw 'em." Clarke was unperturbed and as always, he was watchful.

"I'll try," said Frank. "See you later." He threw a nod to Ken Martin and left the saloon.

Outside, the world was swimming with an excess of dirty water. Over the steady sound of rain came a louder, more insistent roar. It was the river swollen now to a violent torrent that threatened to leave its banks any second. He walked through the roiled air as far as the hotel, went up to his room and changed his shirt; there was a flung-back streamer of Cal Given's blood across the front of it. He then washed his face, bathed his aching hands, and went down to the hotel dining-room. It was then a few minutes past noon.

He did not expect to see Belle there, yet she was waiting, and as far as Frank could see even her feet were dry.

He went to her table and hesitated. She said gravely, "Join me, Frank." Then she noticed the marshal's badge and her eyes swept back to his face. "What happened?"

He sat, dropping his hat to the floor beside his chair. "Two more shots taken at your brother. I reckon you heard them."

"Yes; I saw him leave his horse in the middle of the road and run into the livery barn, too."

"What was Clarke doing?"

"Sitting out there in the rain on his horse looking for someone to shoot. He didn't fire though."

"Did you see where the shots came from, Belle?"

"No; but Luke wasn't hurt. He came out of the barn like a grizzly bear heading for the saloon. How did you get Cal's badge?"

113

"Your brother gave it to me. Given and I tangled a while back. When Luke came in Given was just coming around. Your brother took Given's badge and gave it to me."

She looked at him with that same expression she had worn the day before at the emporium; like she wanted to trust him but could not. He read the expression right and quirked a mirthless smile at her. "Take a chance," he said softly.

"What?"

"What you're thinking about me. Take a chance."

She gave him a keen glance, arrested by what he had said. Before she could speak, if indeed she had intended to, he pushed his advantage over her.

"Why has Luke so many enemies?"

She became instantly defensive. "Everyone has enemies. You ought to know that; you've certainly gone out of your way to make them since you came to Pioche."

He shrugged. "None that've tried to pot-shoot me. Why, Belle? What's Luke done?"

"Stood up for his rights," she said, and looked around for the waitress, impatience and distaste arching her eyebrows and thinning her lips.

"What rights?"

"Frank; you're marshal here, not prosecuting attorney or judge."

"I don't often judge men," he said slowly, wondering how near the truth he was skirting. "I reckon I'll give Luke back the badge. I can't serve a man I don't know anything about."

"Does your gun have a conscience?" she asked coldly.

He caught her eyes and held them. "It has a conscience, yes."

His words seemed to work through her. She said no more until their orders had been taken, then she put both elbows on the table and cupped her hands beneath her chin and studied Frank's face. "All right, Marshal, I'll tell you. You're Luther's man now; I suppose you'll have to know enough to protect his interests."

"And yours."

"Yes; and mine."

"Shoot then, I'm listening."

"We came to Pioche from California. Luther made a lot of money in the goldfields."

"Mining?"

"Gambling. We bought three ranches here. That gave us complete control of the upper Meadow Valley range." Her eyes wavered. "There was some opposition at first, but it didn't amount to much."

Frank's head came up slowly. His eyes were unusually bright but he said nothing and Belle went on speaking.

"Of course Luke made enemies. He's a forceful person; always has been."

"Pretty forceful if folks take to shooting at him."

"All right, have it your way. He has enemies and he uses other men. But he's getting rich and there's no other way to do it."

"How about you?"

"I had some money. I put it in with his to buy those upriver ranches."

"And block off the range?"

"Yes. You say that as though it's a crime to control cattle range."

"Depends on how you do it, Belle."

Their meal came and for a few moments neither of them spoke again. Then Belle said, "Frank; Cal Given told me you had a brother named Jess Harrison."

He had been expecting this and he blandly smiled at her now. "Be pretty hard to do with a name like Baer."

She did not speak again until near the end

of the meal but it was obvious that her attention remained upon him. Presently she drew back and looked out the window where rain was still pouring down with an unrelenting monotony. "You could make a good life here, Frank." Her eyes switched back to his face. "On your own terms," she added tenderly, reaching over to lay a hand upon his arm with the pressure of fingers speaking for her, using her smoky gaze to send its promise and its warmth against him, holding him in limbo across the table with the unseen, suddenly revealed passion which came so powerfully out of her.

Gazing strongly upon the perfection of her features he had no sense of triumph. The face of his dead brother intervened and he stood up knowing a mingling of two sensations; longing and regret. He left her without a word, striding out into the dying day.

Chapter Nine

GEORGE and Will Harrison were waiting that night as near the deadfall cottonwood as they dared get, with the river crested and boiling only a short way behind them, and the footing treacherous within a hundred feet of the crumbling banks. Both were attired in raincoats – called "ponchos" by range men – and both were impatient, even after Frank arrived at the rendezvous, to return to town and get out of the fully falling rain.

Before Frank could speak George Harrison said, "He couldn't do it so I had to."

Frank looked from one to the other of them. "Why not, Will? Why couldn't you take the shot at him?"

"Frank," the tallest brother said swiftly, "I ran into one of the drivers from my Carson City office here in Pioche. I didn't dare let him out of my sight for fear he'd tell someone who I was. I had a hell of a time. He left on the evening stage but before he left I was sweating bullets."

Frank nodded and dismissed the subject. "One of those things," he said. "I wondered, when that second shot came, who fired it because you were still in the saloon. All right; now listen you two. Chandler's off Cal Given. I didn't plan for things to work out this way but they did, so that's that." He frowned. "George; our notion that he might get suspicious of Martin too, fell through, but I've got another idea." He looked at Will. "Tomorrow you go hunt up a young feller named Charley Bemis – he took that first shot at Chandler today."

"All right," Will exclaimed. "What about him?"

"Get him to give you a six months' lease on his upriver ranch. Tell him you've got a big bunch of cattle you want to bring into the valley."

Will nodded but George Harrison spoke through a growing frown. "That'll get around town, Frank. Someone might take a pot-shot at Will."

"It's pretty thin ice," Frank conceded, "but we've got to draw Chandler out." He watched the older man's frown deepen. "George; we've got to get him out in the open. Listen; I'm the law in Pioche now and I'll keep an eye on Will. The first raw move Chandler or anyone else makes I'll throw 'em into jail."

"How'll you hold 'em there?" George asked sceptically. "Chandler has twenty riders and there are only three of us." He wagged his head doubtfully. "Frank; you don't have eyes in the back of your head. They'll try to bushwhack Will."

The youngest Harrison spoke up. "Frank's right, George. We've got to get Chandler to make a move or we'll be hanging around here next Christmas. Frank? Where do I find this Charley Bemis?" Frank told him and Will moved off at once towards the path.

"Will," Frank called. "What name you using."

"Mike Rhodes."

"Another thing, Will. After you get the lease stay close to the Cattlemen's Club where I can see you."

Will grunted assent and went forward through the rain. George watched him disappear then turned to Frank. "I've got misgivings about this," he stated. "What am I to do?"

"Sit by that front window in your room with a gun in your lap. Watch the roadway. If anything happens I'll see to it that it breaks out in the middle of the road. The first man to pick off is Chandler's two-gun man."

They left the river when Frank finished speaking and separated at the edge of Pioche. Frank was nearing the hotel when Doctor Pierce materialised out of a dark doorway softly hailing him.

"Given is out to kill you," Pierce said swiftly. "I think you made a bad mistake today."

"Someone else told me that, too," Frank said. "All right, Doctor, thanks for the warning."

By dawn of the following morning the rain stopped. In its wake was a sodden countryside and a cowed town. Over the stillness of emerging life the river's sullen roar permeated every room and store. It was even audible in the hotel dining-room where Frank breakfasted.

Outside a leaden sky hung low but in the east there was a thin red slash where the sun was breaking through. Frank walked the full length of Pioche and back again. He encountered only two people, both merchants, and because he was wearing his jumper neither of these men saw the badge. He wondered how Chandler would explain his high-handedness in replacing Cal Given as Pioche's law officer. The answer he thought, lay in what Ambrose Pierce had said about the people fearing Chandler more than respecting him. Two riders went slithering up the roadway covered from neck to knee by bright yellow ponchos. Neither looked his way; both were concentrating on their horse's footing. Over at the livery barn the proprietor came out and cast a critical stare skyward. Lowering his gaze he met Frank's eyes and called over: "She's over with, thank the Lord," then he waddled back into the barn and Frank entered the Cattlemen's Club where one solitary barman was dusting backbar shelves with a huge turkey-feather duster.

The sky brightened gradually; almost, Frank thought, reluctantly, as the day wore on, and Pioche was too preoccupied with digging out and cleaning up to pay much attention to other things. It was in fact the quietest day Frank had experienced since first riding down into the valley.

In the afternoon Will came into the saloon alone. He ordered an ale and ignored Frank until the barman said, "Guess a lot o' you boys got caught out on the range, eh?"

Will drained his glass and smiled. "Not me. Maybe next year I'll get it when I have my cattle in the valley, but not this year."

Frank understood; Will had seen Bemis and had gotten the lease. The bartender's reaction was different. He stared. "You bringin' cattle into the valley?" he asked quickly.

"Yep. Just leased the Bemis place."

Frank hid a smile at the barman's sudden start. "The *Charley* Bemis place behind Rafter C?"

"Yeah." Will pushed his glass forward. "How about a refill." He glanced along the bar at Frank. "Join me, stranger?"

Frank pushed his glass forward too. The barman was busy a moment then he leaned on the bar bending a long, intent look at Will. Finally he said, "Mister; I've seen you around for the past week – but I reckon you been taken in. Rafter C's got all that land upriver."

"Not the Bemis place," Will said, and tapped his jumper pocket. "I got that. I got a signed lease right here to prove it."

The barman gazed sideways at Frank and caution settled over his face. "Well," he mumbled, "I wish you luck. When you figure to bring your cattle in?"

"I figured to do it within the next few days, but after that rain I'll have to hold off until the ground's dried out a little." Will's broad smile beamed. "Seven hundred head and six riders."

Frank saw the barman's eyes cloud over as he nodded and moved farther along the bar. The first Rafter C man who comes in, he thought, will get a juicy bit of information to carry back to Luke Chandler. With the ironic humour still lying in his eyes Frank took his glass of ale to a table near the door and sat down.

Will continued to drink at the bar for a while, then he crossed the room with long strides, cast a wink in Frank's direction and passed from sight beyond the doorway. The bartender immediately threw a significant look the length of the room to Frank and made a funereal head-shake. "Some fellers look for trouble," he philosophised, "and some fellers just plain walk into it." He would have said more but something beyond the doorway caught and held his attention. Cal Given pushed in off the plankwalk and started forward without at once seeing Frank; did not see him in fact until he was loosening at the bar, then in the backbar mirror he sighted the steady stare and stillness of the green-eyed man across the room. Given's bruised face paled; his shoulders drew up a notch and stiffness ran out through him. "Whisky," he said in a soft call, and looked away when it came. "Another one." He drank that one off neat also, then he turned and in a steady falling tone said, "Baer – step out into the roadway."

Frank was slow in replying. "Look under this table," he said softly. "Go ahead, Given; bend down and look under this table."

Given did not have to; it was not a new trick. He knew the cocked gun was trained on him out of sight there. He swallowed visibly.

"Put your gun on the bar, Given."

"Like hell!"

Frank's head inclined the slightest bit. "All right; then fill your hand."

"Not like this I won't."

"Given," Frank said icily. "I'd just as soon shoot you like this as any other way. Put it on the bar or use it!"

"I got a witness, Baer, if you shoot me now."

Frank eased off the hammer beneath the table and re-cocked it. The snippet of sharp sound carried cannon-loud through the stillness. The barman was frozen motionless. Someone hammering across the road somewhere made an echo which came suddenly, jarringly, into the hush of the saloon.

Frank said, "I don't care about your witness, Given. I'm the law in Pioche now; *I* say you are resisting arrest."

Given's eyes widened; there was a faint tic

at the corner of his mouth. He reached down very carefully, drew his six-gun and put it upon the bartop. Frank arose, holstered his gun and jerked his head sideways. "Outside," he ordered.

"No!" Given blurted out. "Not unarmed!"

"I'm arresting you," explained Frank, "not killing you. Now move!"

Given moved finally, shuffling across the room. At the door Frank joined him; when he paused to cast an imploring look at the bartender Frank gave him a hard shove and Cal Given stumbled out on to the plankwalk.

They crossed through ankle-deep mud to Pioche's Marshal's office and there Frank locked his predecessor in a strap-steel cell. As he tossed the key upon the table he said, "Given; you had just one friend in this town. Now you don't even have him."

"Don't fool yourself," the prisoner said heatedly. "He'll make you turn me loose."

Frank nodded thoughtfully. "He might at that. You know a lot about him, Given. He just might want you out in the open at that." Frank walked to a chair and sat down. He took out his gun and began a very methodical inspection of it. From across the room Cal Given watched him.

"He'll skin you alive for this, Baer."

Frank made no reply. When he finished with the gun he made a cigarette and smoked it lounging against the wall and ignored Given.

"If I'm not out of here when he gets to town today you'll wish you'd never been born, Baer."

Frank hitched himself up a little in the chair. "No hurry," he said lazily. "Luke won't be in until nightfall. Maybe he won't even get here then, the way the roads are." He smiled thinly at Given. "It won't make any difference anyway. I got my orders, Given."

"What orders? Are you trying . . ."

"To let you escape," Frank improvised. "Let you get out into the roadway where everyone can see you running; then cut you down."

Given put both hands on the steel straps; his knuckles whitened from pressure and he stared at Frank, who held his thin smile.

"See how it works, Given? The barman can testify I arrested you. No one but you'n me'll know I let you out of that cell. No one'll know you're runnin' for your life. All they'll know is that I shot you in the roadway." Frank blew out a great gust of smoke. "Shot while trying to escape. It's an old dodge and it always works. No one'd know that better than you."

Given gasped a falsetto cry. "You dassn't. I won't run."

"That's no problem," Frank said smoothly. "It might even be better to do it in here. I can put a gun in your hand – afterwards. When you're dead it'll be just my word." He looked carefully at his cigarette. "I think I like that better anyway, come to think of it."

Given's face glistened, his lips turned quaveringly slack. He forced a heartiness. "All right, Baer," he said with false camaraderie. "You can have her. I'll saddle up and ride on. She didn't want me anyway."

Frank ground out the cigarette and thumbed back his hat. "Hell," he said scornfully, "I've got her anyway. No, Given; I got this other little job to take care of for Luke."

"I don't believe you!"

"You don't have to. I don't care about that and neither does anyone else. You're cooked, Given. Cooked to a fare-thee-well. You shot your last man in the back."

Given collapsed under the strain; sat

down all loose and shaking. Frank watched him over an interval of dead silence then spoke. "You must know a lot to be worth more to Luke dead than alive. 'Course, you played your cards all wrong too, trying to get Luke and the others down on me over Belle."

"Belle," Given croaked. "I wish I'd never seen her. Wish I'd never seen Luke too, and Ken, and all of them." He looked out at Frank in sudden desperation. "Baer; I'll give you a thousand dollars to look the other way while I ride off. A thousand cash."

Frank got up, crossed to the cell and stood looking down. "I don't need your money, Given. I'm not sure I'd let you ride out anyway."

"What . . .?"

"I think you're a murderer. If you're not you know . . ."

"No by God!" Given sprang up and held to the bars of his cell. "I never murdered anyone and that's the Gospel truth."

"Who did?"

"Murdered who?"

"Jess Harrison."

Cal Given's mouth snapped closed. After a moment of staring he whispered, "By God! I was right, wasn't I? You *are* kin to him."

"Who killed him, Given?"

"Will you let me out . . .?" It trailed off in a steadily diminishing tone as Frank drew and cocked his short-gun.

"Who, Given?"

"Ken. Ken Martin took two of the riders and went out there when Harrison wouldn't sell and wouldn't move off. It was Ken; I swear it was."

Frank put up the gun staring steadily at his prisoner, remembering Ken Martin's cold eyes behind their heavy dark lashes, remembering Martin's unmistakable look of cruelty and contempt. "What were the names of the other two men?"

"Sam Rush and Idaho Carson."

Frank turned away, walked as far as the doorway then faced around. "Everybody in Pioche gives advice," he said. "I'm going to give you some, Given. I'm not alone. I'm going to lock this door so no one can come in here, and if you try to call out and warn Chandler – you'll be killed. Understand?"

"Yes. I won't say anything, Baer. You got my word on it."

Frank's lips curled. He scooped up the keys off the table, passed out into the roadway, locked the office door and started up the plankwalk with bitterness eating at his brain like an acid.

An empty stage coach was pulling away from the hotel. Frank crossed through the mud unheedingly and entered the lobby. The clerk cast him a brief and harassed look then turned away. He heard the people and he saw them but until he reached the stairs they made no impression upon him. Then a set of fingers brushed across his arm and he paused. It was Charley Bemis. He jerked his head sideways and moved into a shadowed corner. Frank followed. When they were secluded Bemis said, "Did you send that tall feller to me?"

"I did. What about it?"

"Just wanted to be sure is all."

Frank started away.

"Wait a minute," Bemis said sharply. "That ain't all." Frank waited. "When Luke finds out what I did he'll send his two-gun man calling. I want protection."

"All right," said Frank evenly, "you'll get it. Stay in your shack tonight with the door barred. I'll come down there when I get the time." He watched the younger man's face a moment, then said, "Thanks. I think this'll help," then he continued on up the stairs without looking back.

He went to room Number Ten and lifted the latch. It was not locked but he made only two forward steps when a gun cut hard over his kidneys, and almost as suddenly was withdrawn. "If you'd lock the damned door," he said bleakly, "you wouldn't have to do that."

George moved away, back towards a chair near the window which overlooked Pioche. "What're you doing here in broad daylight?" he demanded.

"Chandler's foreman and two Rafter C riders killed Jess."

George Harrison turned for a long look at Frank. He said nothing.

"I've got Cal Given in the jailhouse. He told me that."

George returned to his vigil of watching the town. "All right," he said finally in a matter-of-fact tone. "Now, how about Will?"

"He got the lease. I just saw Bemis. He's shaking in his boots over what he's done. I said I'd protect him."

"Better concentrate on protecting Will," the older man muttered, frowning down towards the roadway. "I've got a bad feeling about this mess, Frank. If you can prove Martin and those other two did it, why don't you wire outside for a U.S. Marshal?"

Frank crossed to the bed and sank down. "By the time a federal lawman could get here," he answered, "it'll all be over."

George looked around. "What's in your mind?"

"The other two men are named Carson and Rush. I don't know either of them by sight. That's the first thing I've got to do. After that I want to meet all three of them at the same time."

"Don't be silly," exclaimed George Harrison. "There's that two-gun man also, remember. And there's Luke Chandler."

Frank looked up. "You take care of the two-gun man from this window, George, when hell busts loose. I'll call them when they're in plain sight out in the road."

"If you get the chance," George replied, looking away again. "Listen Frank; we haven't taken our time over this to have you blow up now and act hot-headed like Will. We're older men, you and me; remember that or none of us will get out of Pioche alive."

"I'll remember," Frank said, arising. "I just wanted you to know, George. Jess's killers are named Idaho Carson, Sam Rush, and Ken Martin. Pass that along to Will when you get the chance. If one of us goes down the others'll want to remember."

He left his brother's room and descended the stairs. The lobby still had people milling around. He edged through them and returned to the roadway. There was a cold bite to the early evening and faint-glowing lamplight shone off dozens of murky puddles out in the churned roadway.

Chapter Ten

IT was afternoon of the following day before Chandler rode into Pioche and meanwhile Frank had hit upon a novel idea for protecting Charley Bemis. He had the nighthawk locked in the Marshal's office ostensibly to guard Cal Given, but also as a means for keeping him out of sight of the Rafter C. It worked; when Chandler heard that Bemis had leased his ranch he sent Dan Clarke to find him while he and Ken Martin waited in The Cattlemen's Club for the man he had leased to. Frank was there; he had sent Will upstairs shortly before the Rafter C came to town to warn George of their coming. He had also told Will to stay with George until he sent for him.

Chandler was of course incensed that a stranger had leased land in the heart of his range, but he was not particularly troubled. As he told Frank: "This feller doesn't know what he's doing. When he finds out he'll hit the trail."

"And if he doesn't?" asked Frank.

Chandler's dark eyes smiled. "Then he'll get a little help on his way. Say; have you seen Cal Given around today?"

"Not lately," answered Frank, "but he's around. You can't get rid of a bad penny."

Chandler leaned on the bar. "I might have to though," he said, examining the glass in his fist. "Been something in the back of my mind these last few days." Frank said nothing and Chandler switched the subject. "That feller Harrison still in town?"

"Yes."

Chandler nodded. "I think he got to Given some way. Probably with cash. And I can't have Cal shootin' off his mouth."

"What about?"

"About a lot of things. But that's not the point right now."

"What makes you think he sold you

out?"

"Listen, Baer; Given and Ken and I made a plan to get rid of this Harrison. That same night Given says someone hit him and warned him he'd die if anything happened to Harrison." Chandler looked up. "Now; no one but we three even knew we planned to get rid of Harrison." Chandler paused a moment for effect, then added: "Now; how does that look to you?"

Frank flagged the barman for ale, then he said, "I can't see a man slugging himself, Chandler. It doesn't make sense."

"It'd make sense for, say, a thousand dollars." Frank got his ale and sipped it a moment as Chandler spoke. "Cal's not a real trustworthy person, you know."

"I don't know," Frank said, holding the glass near his lips. "But I'd say if anyone slugged Given it was you or Martin."

Chandler's head came up. He glanced farther along the bar where Martin was talking to the bartender, then returned his gaze to Frank. "That's silly," he growled.

"Yeah? Maybe; but like you said – a thousand dollars is a lot of money." Frank put the glass down and still did not look at Chandler. "Listen; if only the three of you knew about the plan to roust Harrison – and if you didn't slug Given – who did?"

Chandler scowled. "He did it to himself, I told you."

"Bunk. Try slugging yourself in the jaw, Chandler." Frank turned to lean upon the bar and gaze out over the room. People were milling around the tables, conversation was loud and constant. Nearby Frank, Chandler was turning his glass around and around. On Frank's far left Ken Martin was drinking with some cowboys. Through the grey atmosphere Frank saw Dan Clarke swing in off the plankwalk and start through the crowd towards the bar. He waited with an impassive face and a flutter in his chest for Clarke to report on Charley Bemis. Someone played the saloon's music box and Frank could not hear what was being said less than six feet from him. He turned in time to catch Chandler's glance.

"Who you got in the jailhouse?" Chandler demanded.

"A fighting drunk," Frank said easily, gazing past at the two-gun man, "and a singing drunk. Why? You want 'em let out?"

Chandler ignored the question. "Dan couldn't find that weasel of a Bemis."

"I saw him around town this morning,"

Frank said truthfully.

Clarke heard and spoke up. "Maybe you did, but he ain't around now."

Chandler drummed on the bar-top. "Something wrong here," he growled. "Dan said he went to Given's place and he hasn't been there since yesterday."

Frank allowed an interval of silence to pass then he said, "Maybe they sloped; the two of 'em."

Chandler continued to drum with his fingers and scowl. He was silent. Beyond him Dan Clarke motioned to the bartender, got a drink of rye and downed it. Then he thumbed back his hat and turned to gaze disinterestedly over the room.

Ken Martin came up, studied each face in turn then said to Chandler, "What's wrong?"

Chandler made no answer so Frank said, "Given and Bemis have disappeared."

Martin pushed in beside Chandler. "Harrison probably bought 'em off," he said.

Chandler's dark gaze lifted. "Does he have that kind of money, Ken?"

Martin was puzzled and Frank, his greeny eyes emerald hard and sheathed, bored into Martin too. The range-boss slowly straightened off the bar. "How in hell

138

would I know?" he said to Chandler. Then: "Say, what's got into you, Luke?"

Chandler turned to Clarke. "This Harrison is in room ten at the hotel. Go up there, pick a fight and down him."

Clarke said, "Now?"

"Right damned now!"

Clarke started towards the door. Frank watched him go; it was difficult not to show the alarm inside him. Chandler's voice cut across his urgent thoughts. "Baer; let's see how good you are with a gun too," he said. "Go hunt up that feller who got Bemis's lease."

Frank said "All right" as casually as he could and drew away.

"When you find him – hide the body," Chandler ordered.

Outside, day was swiftly fading before a fresh curdling of dark clouds. Frank hesitated briefly to see if Martin or Chandler were following him and when no one appeared he cut rapidly northward along the plankwalk towards the hotel. He was passing the doorway when two reverberating gunshots quivered in the air and across the lobby two men at the desk, one the clerk, started violently. Frank went up the stairs two at a time palming his handgun. At the first-floor landing he twisted to the left, then slowed and stopped. Dan Clarke was lying on his back across the hallway. Both his pistols lay near the body.

"Hello, Frank?"

It was Will standing wide-legged quietly gazing through the gloom to where Frank had stopped. He holstered his gun and bobbed his chin towards the two-gun man.

"They say in his business you aren't allowed any mistakes. I guess he was careless. He knocked on the door. When I opened it of course I had a gun in my hand. He didn't have, but he went for 'em so I shot him."

Frank went closer. "They heard those shots all the way to Carson City," he hissed. "You beat it out the back way and go to the rendezvous."

"Why? You're the law an' it was a fair . . ."

"Shut up and do like I say," Frank snapped, giving his brother a shove along the corridor. Will moved then, swiftly and unerringly towards the back stairway and Frank pushed farther into the room. "George," he barked. "You shot him."

The elder man stared, naked six-gun dangling in his fist. "Me?"

"Yes. He came to the door and knocked and you shot him."

"Why?"

"Chandler sent him to kill you. Do you understand that?"

"Certainly I understand it. What of it?"

"You damned fool; he'll send someone else now, so I'm arresting you. I'll lock you up. The jailhouse is the only safe place for you now, believe me."

George considered this and very gravely held out his weapon. "Then let's go," he said.

When they got downstairs there was a clutch of curious people milling around in the lobby. Frank ignored all of them except the clerk. "Get someone to haul the carcass to Doc Ambrose's embalming shed," he said, and pushed George out into the thickening night.

He knew it would be a matter of moments before Chandler heard about Dan Clarke and he wanted George securely locked up by then. They crossed the roadway and went south as far as the Marshal's office and there Frank unlocked the outer door and drove his brother inside. Charley Bemis was standing motionless in the centre of the room with a cocked shotgun in both hands.

141

"Point that thing some other direction," growled Frank, and barred the door from within.

Bemis lowered the gun. His brows drew down. "That's your other brother, isn't it?" he asked.

"You tell him," Frank instructed George. "Now listen you two; keep that door barred from inside and I'll lock it from outside. I don't care if the President of the United States wants you to open it – don't do it."

"Frank . . .?"

"No time for talk now, George. There are plenty of riot-guns in here and if you get lonesome there's Given to talk to," he shot a look at the wide-eyed, motionless man behind the bars, then moved towards the door. "I'll see you later. Remember what I said – don't open that door for anyone but me."

He left them standing uncertainly in the guttering lamplight and re-crossed through the mud towards the saloon. Ken Martin emerged as Frank stopped on the far plank-walk to kick the weight off his boots. He was alone. Frank said, "Where's Chandler?"

"Went down to his sister's place right after you left. Some feller just busted in

142

here hollering Clarke got shot."

"He did." Frank's steady gaze stayed on Martin's face. His face was impassive, but threateningly so. "Harrison shot him at the hotel."

"Harrison? He's a banker not a . . ."

"You think you'n Dan Clarke are the only ones around who can use guns?"

Martin did not answer. He was having trouble believing a middle-aged banker had out-shot a professional gunman. "Well," he finally said, "where's Harrison now?"

"Why? You want to try your luck?"

Martin heard again the thin harshness of Frank's tone and his brows drew down. "Baer; are you tryin' to ride me?" he asked.

Frank's face swiftly darkened. His brain seemed filled with a sudden terrible hatred but his voice, instead of rising whip-like, came out so low it was scarcely audible. "Ride you, Martin? I wouldn't touch you with a ten foot pole – unless you made me."

The range-boss drew upright stiffening there in the saloon's half-light. He seemed to really see Frank for the first time. "I always had my doubts about you," he exclaimed. "Maybe Cal wasn't too far off after all."

"The only thing Given was right about,

143

Martin, is that I beat his time with Belle. Now go on back in there and drink up."

"That sounded like an order," Martin said, lowering his head a little, dropping his shoulders.

Frank took a long step forward. He was very close to Chandler's foreman. "It was an order," he said, and caught Martin's shirt drawing the range-boss too close for him to use his gun. "You disobey and you go to jail."

Martin's eyes were more puzzled than angry. "What's got into you, Baer? You crazy?"

Frank straightened his arm suddenly flinging Martin reelingly backwards. "Draw," he called after him.

The foreman fetched up against the saloon wall and became very still. Frank waited. Moments passed in heavy silence where they faced one another but Martin made no move towards his gun. "I don't mind killin' you, Baer, but first I want to know why you're forcin' a fight."

Frank's lips drew down. "You won't fight," he said. "You won't fight anyone face to face, Martin." He went ahead, pushed himself very close and lifted the range-boss's gun from its holster and poked

Martin with it. "Walk," he ordered. "Head for the jailhouse." Martin would have spoken but he winced instead from the muzzle of his own gun.

When they were across the road and moving south Martin found his voice again. "You're insane, Baer. Luke'll have your hide for this."

Frank rapped with Martin's pistol on the door then unlocked it and called out softly. From within came sounds of the bar being gratingly raised. Frank pushed Martin inside and kicked the door closed behind them. At Martin's sharp exclamation of surprise at seeing Given, George Harrison and Charley Bemis, Frank said, "All your old friends, Martin. George; this is Jess's killer."

The elder Harrison came forward. "What's his name?"

"Ken Martin."

George swung a big arm and Martin had no time to get clear nor defend himself. He crumpled and lay still with George standing over him. "Why didn't you kill him, Frank?"

There was a crushing silence before George was answered. "Later maybe. Right now I've got to go see Will. George; you and

Bemis lock him up with Given. Be sure he has no hideout weapons. He's the kind to carry 'em."

Frank gestured for Bemis to bar the door after him and left. Darkness, accentuated by the build-up of clouds overhead, lay over Pioche. Frank stood in deep shadows for several minutes watching the roadway. There was no sign of disturbance so he finally struck out south towards the river. When he found Will the latter was smoking his fifth cigarette and looking black as thunder.

"What in the devil kept you?" he demanded, on sighting Frank. "I been down here long enough to make a saddle."

Frank told him. Will's dark look faded. "Chandler'll miss Martin and he'll wonder about George."

"I don't aim to give him time to do either, Will. I'm going to his sister's house, where he is right now, and arrest him too."

"I'll go with you. Maybe we can pull out of this doggoned valley now." Will threw down his cigarette and stamped it. "I want first crack at Martin, though."

Frank shook his head. "You go back uptown and get atop the jailhouse with your carbine. I think I'll be able to take Chandler without any trouble, but if there is any you be ready. When I get back with Chandler you come down. If I don't get back . . ." Frank shrugged. "Let George out of there and you two make a run for it."

"All right," Will said agreeably. "*After* I kill Martin!"

Frank strode north along the river until he came to the western terminus of the roadway where Belle Chandler's house stood. Then he walked easterly towards Pioche's main thoroughfare and paused at Belle's little picket gate.

There was a flashy chestnut gelding at the hitchrail. It eyed Frank with serene unconcern. Beyond, even in the dim light, Belle's house shone whitely and there was lamplight pouring from the windows. Somewhere uptown but clearly audible down here came the solid punching of a running horse passing hurriedly over drying mud. Frank listened until the sound passed beyond recognition and a barking dog across the road covered its last fadings. A number of things crossed his mind; he had not meant to call out Ken Martin, but when the time had come he had been unable to restrain himself. It was a difficult thing to face your brother's murderer; he knew too that only a very thin thread had prevented him from killing the range-boss.

He looked upwards, drew in a big breath and exhaled it starting up Belle Chandler's walkway. He would keep a tighter rein on his temper this time. He would take Luke to the jailhouse. There would be a showdown where his brothers could witness it.

Chapter Eleven

BELLE admitted him but seemed to hesitate as she did so. From behind her a voice called forward: "Luke? Is that you, Luke?"

Frank started past Belle and at the last possible moment she moved aside. He sucked back a big breath expecting to find Luther Chandler but the rugged, grey-eyed man in the parlour was a stranger; at least Frank did not know him by name although he had seen him with the Rafter C riders around town. He stopped with the other man's gaze fully on him and looked around the room. They were alone, the three of them, and Belle, standing back by the door was watching Frank.

"Who are you, mister?" Frank

demanded.

The cowboy's face blanked-over; his mouth went flat to match the coldness in his glance. "Don't take that badge too serious," he said. "All you got to know is that I'm from Rafter C."

Frank considered this briefly then faced Belle. "Where's your brother?"

"He isn't here," she answered, seeing something in his face that rooted her to the floor. "He left a while ago. Why?"

Frank returned his attention to the cowboy. His lids crept closer together. "I'll ask you again," he said in that scarcely-heard, very low voice. "Who are you?"

The rider flushed. "An' I'll tell you again – don't take that badge too serious."

Frank went forward in a sudden lunge. The rangeman raised up on the balls of his feet to whirl away but he didn't make it. Frank caught him in a fierce grip and shook him. "Your name, mister!"

Belle sprang forward. Her tug at Frank's arm might as well not have touched him. "Frank! Leave him alone! Get out of here!" She drummed on him with both fists. "It's none of your business who I entertain in my own home. You're worse than Given. Take your hands off him!"

Frank spun the cowboy away, sent him fetching up against the wall with a shock that rattled the windows. They faced each other crouched and waiting. Belle ran between them facing Harrison. There was a spitting, clawing feline look of fury on her face making it ugly. *"Get out!"* she snarled.

Frank looked past at the rider, whose face had gone pale. "For the last time, mister – your name."

"It's Idaho Carson," Belle flung at him. "Now get out of here or I'll have Luke . . ." It atrophied, drew out into a fading tone that died into the deep hush before the sentence was completed. Belle saw the change sweep over Frank's face; saw its growing deadliness. Outside a horse nickered. No one paid the slightest attention.

"Draw, Carson," Frank invited. "You're lucky; you're getting a chance."

Idaho Carson's curiosity showed through his wariness. "Why? What's got into you, feller?"

"Draw!"

Carson's lips closed, they drew out long. A tawniness showed in his glance. Then he moved. Frank had sensed it coming; he too flashed for his gun. There was only one explosion. Idaho Carson straightened up

150

against the wall, held there by impact. The gun fell from his hand and he stared strongly at Frank. "Why?" he husked. "Why, Baer?"

"Harrison," Frank corrected him, and watched Idaho Carson go slowly down the wall looking up into Frank's eyes. He framed the word "Oh," with lips which had no breath passing them and went forward, a little sideways, and was still.

Belle was turned to stone staring in fascination at the wall where Carson's blood left a long streak floorward. Frank shucked out the spent casing and plugged in a fresh cartridge, then he moved towards the door. It was the movement, the solid sound of bootsteps which brought Belle Chandler around, one hand rising to lie lightly on her chest. She repeated his name so softly it was no more than a faint echo.

"Harrison . . ."

Frank turned. There was bitterness in him. It showed heavily in his expression. He had not meant this thing to happen but a hating man could withstand just so much temptation and no more.

"Given was telling the truth," Belle husked, looking large-eyed up at him. "You *are* his brother."

"So you knew about Jess, too," he retorted bitterly.

"I thought – you were jealous – when you burst in here."

The greeny gaze was icy. "Of you, Belle? No. Maybe there was a time when I could have been, but not now."

She put out a hand to steady herself against the wall. "You'll never get away with this, Frank," she said, in a voice growing momentarily stronger.

He opened the door, passed through and slammed it with a vivid picture etched for ever in his brain of Belle Chandler's face. He turned east beyond the picket gate and walked steadily towards the centre of town. Not until he was nearing the corner did he hear a racing horse, then he stopped and looked back. It was Belle. She was riding the chestnut gelding with her hair and skirt flying and her face twisted with urgency. She shot by him, swung north and fled along Pioche's main thoroughfare. He saw people turn and stare, then understanding came. She knew where Luke was and rode now to warn him. He stood motionless for only a moment then broke over into a run for the livery stable. He had to overtake her; no man living was a match for Luke's Rafter

152

C crew, not at odds of twenty-to-one.

The liveryman watched Frank saddle up and spring aboard. He emerged from his office and stood well back as horse and man spun outward into the night, which lay close now, heavy with rain-scent again. He walked carefully forward and craned his neck but Frank was gone into the blackness; even the sounds of his passing soon died out. The liveryman removed his hat, scratched his head heartily, put the hat back on, shuffled back towards the cone of orange light coming from his office and disappeared beyond the door.

Frank rode with the river's garrulous mutter on his left and the horizon ahead no more than pistol-shot beyond, where night dripped solidly over the retreating land. He felt under him the willingness of his horse to plunge headlong but he held the animal to a long canter and after several miles he slowed to a walk, straining to hear Belle. There came, he thought, a very faint drumming. He angled easterly and lifted the horse into a lope again; rocketed along like that until sixth-sense told him he must be close.

He had no time to reproach himself although the tightness in his belly was attributable to an increasing fear that what he had done, how he had revealed himself, left Will, George, and Charley Bemis, in a very bad position.

Ahead a horse whinnied. He drew swiftly down and wig-wagged the reins to take his own animal's mind off answering. It came to him then, that when he had seen the chestnut gelding in front of Belle's house there had been the jutting butt of a carbine thrusting upwards from beneath a rosadero. He considered the likelihood of Belle Chandler ambushing him. The idea seemed too foreign for acceptance until he recalled the ugliness of her face in wrath, then he sat motionless rummaging the night for movement or sound. There was neither. He waited a full minute then dismounted, led his horse slowly forward to a cottonwood shoot and tethered it there. He had no carbine; never carried one in fact and was known in his own country as a short-gun man. One of those rangemen who carried only a sidearm because they believed in self-protection only.

Around him there was more than stillness. The night was turning warm, muggy with the breath of rain, and the night-burnt land stretched out darkly in every direction. He began a slow approach in the direction

154

of the whinnying horse.

There was a break in the plain. He paused to consider it and although the restlessness within him urged haste, he could not avoid the suspicion that in that arroyo, if anywhere at all, Belle would be waiting with Idaho Carson's carbine. He made a wide detour, cut well above a straggling shallow crevice leading into the deeper break and, placing one foot carefully ahead of the other foot, went pacing forward. He was nearing the deepest part of the gulch when he heard leather slide over gravel. He stopped dead-still with a quick warning flashing out along his nerves. But with the warning came something else; he considered it now, standing stone-still. That noise had been too heavily made to have been the swift grating of a woman's shoe.

He squatted, waiting and thinking. It was entirely possible that Chandler had nightriders out and that Belle had found one of them. The disappearance of Given, Bemis, and Ken Martin too, if Chandler knew of it, gave him excellent reason to be uneasy. Frank grimaced, seeking to sky-line whoever was ahead of him in the arroyo. If Chandler hadn't been in such a hurry to leave Belle's place, he'd have had all the

155

answers by now.

There was nothing to see above the rind of earth, but a second sound of human weight shifting came, as softly secretive as the first sound had been. Frank instantly placed it. He inched forward again, drawing his gun now, holding it forward with a thumb-pad pressed to the checkered hammer.

There remained but one bony outcropping of eroded earth between Frank and the place he knew the ambusher was hunkering. He got to it by going down on all fours. Beyond he distinguished yet again the faint crush of a booted foot moved obviously more in impatience and perhaps a growing alarm, than because the bushwhacker had to change position.

Frank went down flat and pushed his chin into the gravel craning for a look around the earth outcropping. "Are you sure?" a faint voice whispered. He recognised the answering tone instantly. "I'm positive," Belle Chandler said. The man's voice sounded irritable. "Then why don't he come?"

Belle made no answer to that.

Frank sighted their crouched silhouettes. He very slowly pushed his gun-hand forward, tightened his hold on the hammer and drew it steadily back to full cock. It made a sharp clicking sound, as loud in that tense darkness as a cannonshot, which carried well beyond the waiting rider and his companion.

"Hold it," Frank said, seeing the Rafter C man beginning to bunch up. "That's better. Mister; put that carbine down behind you. Now the pistol. That's fine." Frank shifted his attention to the shadow beyond the cowboy. It came suddenly upright, flung around and ran. Frank's gun-barrel swerved, tracked it steadily rising to rest between the shoulders but his trigger-finger never tightened. The man, seeking to take advantage of this diversion dropped flat and scooped up his short-gun. He was twisting, throwing it up when Frank fired. He whipped over off balance and threshed in the dirt. Through the echoing gun-thunder Frank heard a horse running. He got to his feet ignoring that sound, went forward and kicked the injured man's guns farther out, then stood there gazing into a pair of pain-racked eyes as pale as dawn.

"Where's Chandler?" he asked.

The wounded man gasped a curse and struggled to sit up. He was shot through the

157

upper leg. With both hands over the injury he rocked back and forth gasping.

"I asked where Luke Chandler is."

"At the – at the ranch."

Frank raised his head listening. Belle's horse was well beyond hearing now. He looked down again. "What's your name, feller?"

"Hardy Willis. Who're you?"

"Didn't Belle tell you?"

"All she said was shoot the man who was chasing her."

"My name's Harrison."

Willis stopped rocking. His jaw slackened and he looked upwards with clear foreboding. "Harrison . . ."

"Yeah. Did you know Jess Harrison who had a little spread near here?"

"Well," Willis hedged, "not real well. Only to wave to when I rode by his place."

"But you know what happened to him all right."

"I know that," Willis said in a fading way and looked down again. "But I had no hand in it."

Frank holstered his gun and made a cigarette. After he lit it he offered it to the wounded rider. Willis took it muttering, "Thanks." Frank made one for himself and smoked a moment before speaking again.

"Belle's going to tell Luke who I am, and Luke's going to round up his crew and head for town."

"Yeah," Willis assented, making a tourniquet of his belt and drawing it up around the bleeding leg. "An' if I was you, Harrison, I'd get out of Meadow Valley as fast as I could because if Luke don't get you Dan Clarke or Ken Martin will."

Frank smiled. "Dan Clarke is dead," he said, "from two bullets. One in the head, one in the chest. And don't worry about Ken Martin either, Willis; he's not around any more."

The Rafter C man's eyes grew round. He studied Frank for a moment without speaking, then took a long drag off the cigarette in his free hand. "Somebody made a bad mistake," he said finally. "Belle said you was a blow-hard and couldn't use a gun."

"What did you expect her to say, Willis; that you didn't stand a chance?" Frank studied the night briefly. "How far's the ranch from here?"

"No more'n a mile; I think maybe a little less, even."

"And which way will Chandler ride when he heads for Pioche?"

"South, straight as a string. There's a trail, pretty well marked, that cuts across Rafter C range headin' due south. It comes into the road below the old – ah – the old Harrison place."

"One more question, Willis. Will Sam Rush be riding with him?"

"If he takes the whole crew Sam'll be along. Even if he don't I reckon he'll take Sam."

"They're pretty close, eh?"

Willis fidgeted. "Well; Sam's pretty handy," he said, and closed his mouth.

Frank nodded. "I expect he is. Pretty handy at shooting into dead men." He dropped the cigarette and trod on it. "Is that bleeding lettin' up a little?"

"Yes."

"You'll be all right then, Willis."

The cowboy seemed relieved. "Yes; I'll make it," he said.

"I'm going to leave your horse and guns. I think I'll leave you a little advice, too."

"Won't be necessary," the cowboy retorted. "I'm pullin' out as soon as I can get back to the bunkhouse and collect my gatherings."

Chapter Twelve

FRANK rode joggingly north-easterly. Ahead somewhere Belle, he knew, would be electrifying her brother with information about him, and Luke's expression would be something to see; the idea appealed to Frank; he almost smiled over it.

He found the trail Willis had spoken of, and as he had said, it was well marked. He rode across it and swung north again, paralleling it. A warm-water creek, very shallow and unnecessarily wide, came meandering southward with a willow-fringe to mark its more northerly course. Frank rode along close to it; he could not be readily sky-lined by nightriders with the willows standing higher than he was against the obsidian night.

He caught no sight of Belle of course but he could estimate how much time stood between them by the scent of settling dust in the air. Twenty minutes, he thought, no more. He stopped finally where the willows made a westerly bulge towards the trail, unshipped his pistol and sat there sniffing and waiting. Silence hung heavy until, far out, a cow bawled and even more distantly a calf answered. This latter tag-end of sound

161

rode down the night softly.

The range seemed apprehensively still and waiting. As always before a storm there was a thickness to the air, a pressing-down solidness that left its imprint on every square inch of a man's skin. He felt this even as he heard or felt some faint flutter in the night; a vague reverberation as of oncoming horsemen. It grew stronger with a pounding urgency and horseshoes striking gravel gave Frank both a definition of its source and a gauge of its distance from him. He cocked his pistol, backed his horse deeper into the willows and waited.

A minute later he heard the first voice when a rider called back for another horseman to hurry up. Seconds later came the rattle of rein-chains, the creak of un-oiled leather and the purposeful pounding of swift-moving mounts. He cast a final glance ahead where the road went past and raised the gun. He doubted if Chandler had been able to bring his entire crew on such short notice but he would have most of them probably; even if he only had six or eight of them the odds were still too great.

Grouped-up silhouettes rising and falling came out of the darkness bearing past. Now, Harrison thought, now! He fired and a leggy bay horse went down without a struggle. One moment the rider was forging ahead, the next moment he was riding straight down into the ground.

Harrison's second shot dumped another mount. This one pinwheeled flinging the rider clear in cartwheel fashion all arms and legs and a whipped-out cry. Someone roared a curse and there was a sound of two riders colliding. Frank saw a blue-red flash of light blossom, then another, and a third. He spun his horse and fired towards the first flash. Chandler's group choked the trail slamming down to a halt in noisy confusion. Other guns threw out daggers of quick light and Frank, loping steadily northward continued to fire at each gun-flash until his weapon was empty. He rode without hurry, re-loading by feel, watching the gunfire cut willows where he had been and hearing the shouted imprecations.

His horse was unmoved by the firing and bent readily north-westerly around the Rafter C men as Frank opened up on them from a new direction. Now the first man broke away and rode for it, back the way they had all come. A second horseman went after him and a third man, crying "Ambush – Ambush – Get out of here!" expedited the rout which followed.

Frank continued to lope southerly and fire but he was deliberately holding high. When the last of Chandler's men was gone he drew out a ways, re-loaded again and sat perfectly motionless listening and waiting. Someone beyond his vision was alternately groaning and cursing. He listened, thinking this was a trap. There was however, a throatiness to the man's voice, a rising and breaking of sound hard to emulate unless pain-inspired, which kept him from riding off. After a time he left the horse and catfooted it forward.

Seeing but unseen, he came to a dead horse lying across a downed cowboy whose leg was pinned and whose gritted teeth scarcely let his breath, let alone his words, pass ashen lips.

There were several dark mounds against the earth nearby. None moved. He went forward, balancing lightly, warily, and stopped twice to heed the hush and the last time the pinned man sighted him, twisted to watch his shadow come closer, assume substance, become a man with a fisted cocked gun in the blackness. Only the rider's importuning eyes showed at first, then his clamped-down jaw and bitter-held lips. Frank knelt near him seeking a gun; there was none. He looked at the man's face then and only vaguely recognised it as belonging to one of Chandler's riders whom he had seen in Pioche. He holstered his short-gun and studied the dead horse; it was lying on its side with all four legs outstretched. It had, he saw from the wound, died instantly and peaceably.

"Use my lariat," the rider croaked. "I think my leg's busted."

Frank doubted that. The ground here had a three inch cushion of fine dust.

"Where'd the others go?" he asked the horseman.

"Back to the – ranch." The man's eyes showed recognition. "Listen; take me to town an' lock me up if you want to – only get this horse off'n me."

"Was Sam Rush with Chandler?"

"Yeh; he was along." The cowboy jutted his chin towards a dead horse. "He was ridin' that bay. You dumped him first."

"Is he still afoot around here?"

"No. Chandler took him up behind the cantle. Listen, Baer – please pull this horse off'n me."

"I'm in no hurry," Frank said coldly and the cowboy groaned. "Was Belle with you?"

165

"No; she stayed at the ranch."

"Why did they go back?"

"They thought you was a bunch of fellers. Chandler said to. Someone was yellin' it was the soldiers."

Frank stood up, grasped the dead animal's hind leg and slowly strained. The carcass moved lumpily with the resistance of dead-weight. He braced his legs and settled into a greater straining. Very gradually the animal inched away sufficiently for the Rafter C rider to extricate his leg. Frank straightened then, breathing deeply and watching the cowboy. "Is it broken?" he asked.

"Don't know. Hurts like hell though."

"I imagine it does," Frank responded dryly. "Where is your gun?"

"Somewhere," was the gasped and disinterested reply. "I dropped it when I fell. Listen, Baer . . ."

"You listen. There's another hurt man out here. His name's Willis. Hardy Willis. You know him?"

"Yes."

"He's pulling out and you'd better do the same. If we meet again, cowboy, the next time more'n a horse is going to fall on you."

Frank went back to his mount, stepped

across the saddle and swung north-westerly riding in a swift walk into the deepest core of night. He had considered returning to Pioche but had abandoned the idea in favour of harassing Chandler at the ranch. He reasoned that Chandler would eventually head for town, but that his first objective would be the man who was now revealed to him as Jess Harrison's avenger; the man whom he had appointed Town Marshal. The fact that Frank was somewhere on Rafter C range would, he thought, spur Chandler to deadly action. Nor was he wrong. At the same time he made out Chandler's buildings, darker against the earth and squarely set upon the skyline, he also saw a brace of horsemen riding ahead of him towards the ranch. Here, as near he could make out, there was no place to leave his mount nor, for that matter, any willows to hide either of them. He slowed, letting darkness hide him from the riders, and progressed only as far as a pistol might reach.

Chandler's ranch was a sprawl of buildings, unpainted, functionally severe and ugly. There were steady-growing prickles of light showing, barely light enough to reflect off wooden walls. One building was totally dark. He approached this one at a slow walk

167

keeping it between himself and the large main house where saddled horses stood drowsily and where men's voices sounded faintly over the distance. He dismounted, struck a match under his hat, grasped dead grass and fired it. Set the brightening fire against dry, weathered siding and re-mounted. Flame spread hungrily; he continued to watch it until the last possible moment when its flickering growth spread, throwing wild shadows against the blackness. Then he wheeled and rode out and around the ranch again cutting back inward from a southerly direction.

Flames stood straight in the night rising with eager lickings towards the lowering, big-bellied sky. There was at first only one cry from the ranch house, but within seconds other voices sounded and Frank drew rein to watch darting black shapes dance and waver and rush in and out against red-crackling heat. He drew his short-gun, reined at a walk towards the east and when he was within range he fired three times as swiftly as he could raise and drop the hammer.

Pandemonium erupted. Someone cried out a ragged alarm and men scattered throwing aside wet blankets, buckets and spades, in the panic.

Frank's last three shots were sent low through the yard, again in swift succession and he loped south again reloading.

A horseman mounting on the fly careered across the yard, a difficult low-riding target with flames guttering over and around him, and disappeared beyond visibility. A second and third rider dashed away and Frank was reminded of bees leaving a stick-struck hive. He holstered the belt-gun, lifted his own animal into a long lope and struck out south-westerly for Pioche.

Chandler had something to occupy him, at least for a while; he would fight hard to prevent the fire from spreading to his other buildings, and meanwhile Frank would go back, get his brothers out of the town and some way try to find a new hiding place for the prisoners. He had not originally counted on the night for aid but now that he had it there was every reason to think of using it, if possible to offset Chandler's numerical superiority.

He intersected Chandler's trail and later, the Pioche roadway. Not until then did he draw down to listen. Silence smothered every sound; silence as deep and cloying as storm-promise could make it. He continued

169

onward for several miles then circled Pioche and came up towards the jailhouse from the west.

Pioche was not yet abed. It was, Frank estimated, nearly eleven o'clock. The Cattlemen's Club Saloon, for instance, gave off both light and sound, and on the livery-barn-side of the roadway a number of rangemen were lounging in the warm darkness drinking from several bottles and laughing among themselves. Closer, near the intersection which led to Belle Chandler's house, a small and compact shadow shifted from one foot to the other, obviously waiting for some one, or some thing.

Frank left his mount behind the jailhouse and moved towards this last vague outline. He had recognised it as belonging to Ambrose Pierce. There was no sound until he reached out, locked his fingers over the doctor's arm and said, "Not a sound."

Pierce started violently and half swung around. Frank's hold dropped away, and perhaps another time under different circumstances he might have smiled, now he did not.

"What are you doing here?" he demanded.

"Waiting."

"For what?"

"I – don't exactly know. I saw a tall man climb on to the jailhouse roof a couple of hours ago, and I was curious."

"You know what curiosity did for the cat?"

Pierce nodded. "Yes; killed it. But . . ."

"You better go home, Doc. This roadway's likely to become right unhealthy."

"I know who you have locked up in there. A number of people know it by now."

"Well," Frank said laconically. "Pretty busy little town, isn't it? Who is objecting, besides you?"

"No, not me. No one, in fact. There was a call for the Town Council to meet a little while ago. The unanimous decision was not to interfere as long as the Harrisons and Rafter C kill only each other."

"That's nice and neighbourly," said Frank. "Sort of like letting wolves fight among themselves, isn't it?"

"Listen; you'd better let your brother and Charley Bemis out of there. That place is a death-trap." Doctor Pierce canted his head far back. "And – who is that on the roof?"

"Another Harrison."

171

Pierce looked at Frank, suspecting he was joking. Seeing no smile he said quickly, "Good. But you'd better . . ."

"Listen, General Grant," Frank cut in to say. "You go on home now."

"I will. But first, tell me what you're going to do."

Frank's teeth shone in a cold smile. "I can't do that, Doc, because I'm not sure myself. Go on home now and lay out your bandages and carbolic acid. Before this night is over goin' to be a man or two who'll be needing them, I think."

Frank expedited Pierce's departure with a hard shove. He then went to the jailhouse door, inserted the key and struck the panel with his fist. Instantly from within came the sound of a draw-bar being lifted. He was pushing on the door when movement flickered in the other corner of his eye. He dropped, whirled and drew all in one blurry motion.

"Easy," quavered an old voice. "Steady now, boy. You wouldn't want to hurt no old friends."

It was the weasel-faced old man with his constant-cunning smile. Frank straightened part way up with anger mantling his face with dark blood. He swore and the oldster

172

slithered along the jailhouse wall closer ignoring each wrathful epithet.

"If you'll shut up a minute," the old man said, "I'll tell y'something. Couple local fellers rode out a bit ago to tell Chandler who-all you got locked up in there."

Frank said "Thanks; anything else?"

"Yes. There was a couple Rafter C boys in town; they rode south to cut you off from leavin' until Chandler can get here with his whole crew."

"How d'you know that?"

"Was sleepin' in the hay at the livery barn; heard 'em talkin' right next to my stall. One's named Curley Ellis. Other one's Bent Rodger."

Frank brought forth a gold piece and dropped it into an outstretched hand then he entered the jailhouse, slammed the door upon the old man's peering stare, and was nearly blinded by lamplight. But not nearly so blinded that he did not see the array of armament directed straight at him. He made a gesture. "Put that iron away. George; you and Bemis have got to get out of here . . ." There was a solitary knock on the door. As Frank turned George said, "It's Will. Let him in."

Will too was temporarily blinded by the

light. He squinted at Frank. "I thought you were never coming. That's the hardest roof I ever lay on – for so cussed long anyway." He might have said more but George was looking at Frank, his expression settling stubbornly.

"You don't mean leave the prisoners, do you, Frank?"

"I don't think we can make it out with them, George." He told them about Chandler's men south of town and also of the ones who had ridden to Rafter C. Finally, he told them all that had happened since he'd last seen them, and after he finished there was silence.

Will, the least perturbed, looked beyond Bemis and George to the prisoners. He smiled blandly at them. "You boys don't want to miss any of this," he said. Cal Given was thoroughly cowed but Ken Martin's iron gaze was unafraid and uncompromising.

"Don't you worry, feller, I won't forget a bit of it and I won't forget your face either – or the face of . . ."

"Shut up!" Frank snarled, and Martin did not finish his sentence but neither did his hating glance lower.

It was George who spoke now, still

174

obsessed with his idea of keeping the prisoners. "We can split up, Frank. If there's only two of them like you say, probably two of us could make it."

"Maybe," Frank said, making a smoke. "But our only strength it seems to me is in being together, George." He lit up and exhaled as Will spoke.

"How much time we got?"

"Maybe an hour. Maybe more. Chandler'll be plenty busy with that fire for a while yet."

"Then let's you'n me go out, find those Rafter C boys and knock 'em over the head. Then we can ride out with our prisoners, all together."

Frank rejected the suggestion. There was plenty of time, he felt, but not enough to search a town none of them knew well, perhaps engage in a protracted fight in the night, and still escape in a band. He shook his head and gazed steadily at the prisoners before an alternate idea came.

"Will; keep a gun on Given and Martin. George; let 'em out; you and Bemis tie their arms behind them. I think I know how we can avoid being ambushed and get a whack at Luke Chandler too. Hurry up."

Charley Bemis, until now content to listen

and remain silent, leaned upon his carbine and said, "You got any idea how many riders Chandler's got? Close to twenty, Harrison. There's four of us and there isn't a place in this town we can hold 'em off."

Frank heard Bemis out then looked past him towards a little wood-stove in the corner. "Any coffee left in that pot?" he asked.

George replied. "Yes. Frank; did you hear what this boy said? He grew up here remember."

Frank moved towards the stove. "I heard. Get those fellers out of that cell and tie 'em!"

Chapter Thirteen

IT was nearly a full hour after midnight when the first raindrops came, big, fat and heavy. Frank squinted up at the sky. He stood alone under a boot-shop overhang not far south of the livery barn; near the intersection of Main Street and the roadway leading towards Belle Chandler's house. He smoked, studying the sky, hearing the intermittent striking of raindrops and more immediate, the sounds of a town turning gradually from wakefulness to sleepfulness.

In strong blackness he was invisible except when a red glow showed the cigarette burning back under a strong inhalation. He thought that by now Bent Rodger and the other Rafter C man knew they were not going to make a run for it; they would probably be searching for the Harrisons – but very carefully. Normally the idea of two rangemen cat-footing in the night more fearful than forceful might have brought a glint of hard amusement to his gaze; now it did not. In the long hours of this brooding night he had killed one man, shot another and injured a third man. These were not memories a man could live with pleasurably no matter how hard and realistic he was. The night did not help with its increasing drizzle, less powerful than the other rainstorm but equally as depressing. Frank stirred, moved lightly forward to the plankwalk's edge and cocked his head. There was only this soft-constant sound of rainfall. He shot another look at the sky. There was no moon so he could only guess at the time. Along with this speculation came a recapitulation of everything which had happened up to now in Pioche, and of course with each vivid recollection of a narrowly-escaped disaster came hindsight to show what he should have done and how he should have acted. He roamed the roadway with a long and searching stare, saw no movement and went back into the gloom again.

Belle.

He thought of the quickening which had come to him at first sight of her; of large grey-black eyes turned smoky and smouldering and of her fallen defences and her hot kiss. Something had gone out of him here in Pioche; something which left an emptiness. Youth, he thought; it was his youth. He was not a young man in the sense that folks usually thought of a man as being young – in years. But until word had come of Jess's murder he had been many things, he had faced many men under myriad circumstances and until now he had emerged from each challenge unchanged. Now, it was no longer so. Now, it was becoming harder to smile, to laugh, to face life with youth's questing, its interest and its lightness. He thought that this was because of Belle Chandler. He had never before been so strongly drawn to a woman and the disillusionment in discovering that she had known of his brother's killing with no sign of remorse, twisted the knife in his hurting flesh.

He cursed under his breath and looked again into the roadway's glisten. What was keeping Chandler? The fire had not spread; he knew that; so what was keeping him? Certainly not fear – not with as many riders as Rafter C had – then what?

Time passed, the rain continued, and the nightman of The Cattlemen's Club came out across the way, locked the saloon's doors and looked out over the town drawing a coat-collar up against the night's damp chill. He stood a moment breathing deeply, then he turned and went along the plankwalk northerly, head bowed as though bucking a wind although there was no wind at all.

Frank watched him, the only moving thing in Pioche, until he was nearly lost, then he heard the jogging horsemen coming out of the north and a quickening perception came over him; the night took a sharper smell, a brighter darkness and a full meaning.

He stayed well back in the darkness with one hand inches above the graceful sweep of his holstered short-gun. "Come on, Chandler," he said softly into the night. "I think one of us is going to eat crow tonight."

Steadily, without hurrying, the riders slogged into Pioche. They rode grouped, ponchos iridescent with rainshine, their faces death-like beneath hat-brims showing only faintly as curving cheekbones and sunken, shadowed places. Seven of them. No; there were nine. Two more came skittering up from behind and one called forward: "Luke!"

Frank recognised the voice as belonging to Bent Rodger, Chandler's horse-wrangler. The riders all stopped. Rodger pushed on to the lead. "They haven't left," he said quickly, reining close to Luther Chandler, "but we don't know where they are."

"The jailhouse," Chandler said roughly, raising an arm.

"No; the door's plumb open, Luke. You can see inside. Isn't anyone there."

Chandler's arm dropped, his horse mushed forward and the other lumpy shapes followed him. "Did you go inside?" he asked Rodger.

"No – not inside. But you can see in there an' the place's empty."

Chandler said no more until they all stopped facing the Marshal's Office.

"Three, four of you look in there," he ordered. "If it's an ambush those Harrisons're going to wish it wasn't."

Three riders dutifully swung down, sloshed through the roadway and stamped on to the plankwalk. Without hesitating they shouldered into the office and re-emerged almost at once. One of them mumbled: "Empty," and went back to his horse.

Frank watched Chandler's head lift and slowly turn outward, along the north and south run of the roadway. "How do you know they didn't ride out?" he asked Bent Rodger. "They didn't have to follow the road you know."

"We were up on the mountainside until dark," Rodger answered clearly, "an' could see in every direction. After dark we split up and patrolled Pioche out back on the river an' mountain sides o' town. They didn't leave, I'd bet money on that."

Chandler brought his gaze to bear on a slouching rider whose jaws moved steadily, grinding a cud of chewing tobacco. "Sam; take Belle home then come on back. We'll go through here board by board."

Frank watched two riders, one smaller than the other, split off and ride towards him. He flattened deep into darkness

181

straining to see their faces. Under her man's hat Belle Chandler's face was scarcely discernible. The man called Sam, more inured, kept his head up and moving. Frank clearly saw each feature and noted them well; the cowboy's name had a significance for him. Then they turned past and plodded beyond his sight down the sideroad and Frank drew his gun with his attention returned to Luther Chandler.

"All right," Chandler said aloud, his voice turning brisk. "Al, you'n Evan start at the south end of town and work your way north. Search every shed if you have to but make damned sure you either find them or find out where they aren't. Understand?"

Two riders eased away and rode south without speaking. Chandler watched them briefly then said, "Les, you and Bruce start at the north end of town and do the same thing." He hesitated a moment looking at the waiting riders. "A thousand dollars a head for each Harrison – dead if you want it like that; alive if you can't help it."

Frank waited a moment, until the riders had gone on, then he counted the remaining silhouettes; four riders and Luther Chandler. He straightened up off the wall and took one step forward then Chandler was speaking again and he stopped moving.

"Eph; go over to the hotel. That George Harrison feller has a room there. See if he's there."

"An' if he is?" a deep voice asked.

"Shoot him," exclaimed Chandler. "Shoot him a thousand dollars worth and drag the carcass out here in the mud. Go on now."

Frank faded back again.

"Richy!" Chandler barked. "Go on in the jailhouse. I don't think they'll try to get back there, but you wait. Don't light the lamp an' if they come . . ."

"I understand, Boss."

Frank waited until this last rider had dismounted and handed up his reins, then he moved out to the edge of the plankwalk. South of Pioche's heart a dog began barking furiously. Chandler ignored the racket and started for the livery barn. There was a shadowy mounted shape behind him sitting easy in the saddle.

Chandler did not see Frank although he passed within forty feet of him; might never have believed he was there within stones-throw at all if a whipping sound had not come out of the gloom to slap hard against his eardrums.

"Chandler!"

There was no mistaking the meaning, the portent, in that call even though the man who had made it was not immediately visible. Luther Chandler halted with his head moving and his gun-hand diving low.

"Don't try it, Chandler. You too, cowboy. Sit easy now. Real easy."

Chandler still had not distinguished the man-shape from the flooding darkness although he had placed the direction of the voice. He made no move to draw the gun under his hand. Behind him the cowboy, too, was like stone, but he had discovered Frank, had recognised him even in the bad light and was breathing shallowly through faintly dilating nostrils. "I see him," he said to Chandler. "There – by the boot shop."

Chandler squinted briefly then inclined his head the slightest bit. "Yeah. Harrison; you've got about as much chance pulling anything off here in Pioche as a snowball has in hell. Throw down that gun."

"I've got a better idea," answered Frank in a very low voice. "You draw your gun."

"You got the drop," Chandler said, and removed his hand from the pistol butt, laid it in full sight atop the saddlehorn. The shock was gone now; Luther's mind was working clearly, dispassionately. If he could prolong this meeting only a short while longer Sam Rush would ride up the road behind Harrison. Luther nearly smiled. "That was a bad mistake you made," he said to Frank. "You should've lit out when you had the chance."

Frank's face was smooth-drawn and impassive. "Get down," he ordered, "on the left side; either of you make a wrong move and it'll be your last."

The cowboy dismounted first, then Luther Chandler. They stood facing Frank, who beckoned them with his gun.

"Up here. Keep your hands wide now."

As the cowboy reached forward with one foot to step on to the plankwalk Frank spun him, yanked his pistol away and flung it out into the mud. "Now you," he said, facing Chandler. "Turn around." Belle's brother obeyed without a murmur. When he too was disarmed Frank prodded them close. "Around the corner," he said. "To Belle's house."

Chandler paused looking quizzically back at his captor. His faint cold smile broadened; he shrugged and moved off.

Frank herded them up to the hitchrail before the house. There, Luther looked long at Sam Rush's tethered horse and grunted something unintelligible. Frank said, "You thought he'd be coming up behind me." He gave them both a push past the picket gate. "I had other plans for him. Go on in."

There was one lamp burning low on a settee. Behind it, pale except for the deepened blackness of her eyes sat Belle Chandler. Beside her lounging on the same sofa, long legs out-thrust, bold face relaxed, was Will Harrison. Across from him tied by both his arms and legs lay Sam Rush. He twisted bulging-eyed when Luther entered. He would have spoken but at that moment Frank's gun rose, arced high, and came down with a solid meaty sound and the cowboy with Chandler sprawled unconscious just inside the door.

"Tie him," Frank ordered and Will got up. "Where's George and Bemis?"

Will turned as two shadows materialised from beyond the tasselled kitchen entrance, jerked his head at them and continued on forward. Luther ripped out a curse at sight of Charley Bemis. The younger man paled but kept on advancing. Frank said, "Shut up, Chandler. Go sit over there by your sister."

Belle threw a look of strong distaste at

Frank, but he saw more than wrath in her expression; there was a putty-like slackness around her mouth; a fear was in her, he thought. An apprehension of what lay ahead. "Will; when you're finished there roll him over by Rush then go outside by that big tree and wait for the others to come up. Knock on the wall when one comes along."

George Harrison lowered his gun. He and Charley Bemis exchanged a glance and the younger man raised his shoulders and let them drop. "Frank; it might work at that," he said as though apologetic. "I didn't think so at the jailhouse I'll admit."

"It'll work now that we've got Chandler," George chimed in.

Into the ensuing silence came a slight rustle of wind out in the night; it broke the pattern of rainfall briefly then died leaving the constant drumming behind. Frank holstered his gun. "Like I said; Belle's house would be either the first place or the last place they'd come, and even then they wouldn't come expecting to find us here." He considered Sam Rush for a moment. "I expect you know," he said into the upturned face, "who we are by now."

"I know," Rush croaked. "But you ain't

187

got the chance of . . .”

"That's what your boss thought too, but he was wrong." Frank motioned to Bemis. "Prop him up against the wall." When this had been done Frank made a cigarette, lit it and turned his back on the Chandlers. "Rush; have you talked to Ken Martin?"

"No; they got him tied up an' locked in the bedroom."

"That's too bad; I wanted to hear you two blame each other for killing Jess Harrison."

"We didn't have anything to do with it. I swear we didn't!"

"I guess you haven't talked to Cal Given either, have you?"

"No; he left the country or something . . ." Rush's eyes widened slowly. "No," he breathed. "You ain't got him too?"

Frank looked at George with raised eyebrows and the older man nodded. "He's in the bedroom with Martin," he said.

"Rush; Cal Given said you, Ken Martin, and Idaho Carson killed Jess Harrison. Idaho Carson is . . ."

"That's a lie!" The tied man cried sharply. "Ask Chandler there."

Frank went on as though he had not heard. "Idaho Carson is dead. I killed him tonight in this very room. Miss Chandler was here."

Sam Rush was staring hard at Luther Chandler but the owner of Rafter C was watching Frank Harrison.

"I believe Given," Frank said. "So do my brothers. That's too bad for you, Rush. One of us will kill you before this night is over. But tell me something – what did Chandler say to you when he sent you after Jess?"

"He didn't say nothin' because we didn't kill your damned brother."

Frank looked past at George again. "Did you talk to Martin?"

"Yes. He said the same thing Given told you, Frank. The only difference was he didn't mention himself. He said Carson and Rush did the actual killing on orders from Chandler."

Frank looked down with his eyes drawn out narrow against cigarette smoke. "Just you and Carson," he murmured to Rush.

The bound man's face flooded with colour; his cruel lips twisted and he glared at Luther Chandler. "You goin' to try'n pass the buck too?" he demanded. Chandler looked fully into Rush's face and said nothing at all; there was both a warning and a promise in his expression but Sam Rush was beyond heeding either; death was something very real to him at this moment, words no longer held any value at all. He called Luther Chandler a searing name.

"Chandler ordered your brother killed. He told Ken to take me'n Idaho and go over to your brother's place in the night and shoot him. He told us to hang his carcass in the front of the barn where every other rancher who rode by could see it and understand what it meant – for them all to get out of Meadow Valley." Rush's twisted face showed no fear, only a hate which came out of him and went over the room in a hot gust, directed towards Luther Chandler. "Lie your way out of *that*," he cried savagely at Belle's brother.

Frank raised his head after a moment of total motionlessness. "Fetch Given and Martin out here," he ordered, and punched out his cigarette while he waited. Luther Chandler eased forward on the sofa. Beside him, Belle was like stone, only her eyes moving.

"Listen, Harrison; I didn't mean for them to actually kill your brother. All I wanted . . ."

"You rotten liar!" Sam Rush stormed from across the room, silencing Chandler. "Harrison? You get Ken to tell you exactly what was said."

190

Frank straightened up and said, "I aim to, Rush. That's exactly why we're here in Pioche – to get the truth."

A soft but imperative knock came on the east wall. Frank motioned Charley Bemis and George back beyond the tasselled doorway with their weapons then he strode to the door, reached for the latch and glanced over at Chandler. "When I open," he said, "I'll be behind this door, Chandler. You tell whoever it is to come in, and you make it believable because if you don't my brother outside will down your man and I'll get you. Are you ready?"

"I'm ready," Chandler said huskily, and watched Frank's hand tighten and pull. Before the door was fully open Chandler said, "Who is it?"

"Al and Evan, Luke; we combed this danged town from . . ."

"Come in," Chandler called.

Frank's gun-arm raised and fell, raised and fell. "Charley," he called gazing at the tangled, motionless forms. "A couple more for you – how's the rope holding up?"

Bemis approached with George Harrison. He threw a shaky smile at Frank. "Plenty of rope," he said, bending down.

It was Sam Rush who spoke next; there

was contempt more than fright or desperation in his tone. "Luke! you're yellow," he said bitterly. "You're as yellow as a yellow dog. I wish I'd known that six months ago."

Chapter Fourteen

IT was three o'clock in the morning. The rain had dwindled to an occasional light flurry, wind-driven now and actually little more than a strong mist. It was chilly in Belle Chandler's parlour; chilly and damp and unpleasant. George Harrison brought Cal Given and Ken Martin out of the bedroom; pushed them headlong into the front room and watched them gaze at the trussed men, over at Luther and Belle, then raise their eyes to Frank. Of all the impassive faces in that room only Sam Rush's looked less than grim. "Ken," he said to the range-boss, "Luke's wiggling out of the Jess Harrison business." Rush inclined his head towards Frank. "Tell him what really happened."

Martin, all his defiance gone, looked slowly from Luther Chandler to Frank. "I already told this other feller everything there was to it," he said in a slurred, low tone. "Luke sent you'n Carson over there."

Rush swore but Frank was watching Chandler. The rancher's face blanched. "Ken, you fool," he ground out. "What're you trying to do?"

Martin turned sullen, defiant eyes on his employer. "You know doggoned well you ordered it done, Luke."

Belle leaned forward. "Yes, he ordered it done," she spat at Martin. "He ordered *you* to do it. He told you to take Rush and Carson and go over there with them and do it."

Frank said, "Were you at the ranch when he sent them to Jess's place, Belle?"

She did not reply nor even look at Frank; her hot and hating stare was fixed on the range-boss. Frank shifted his attention. "How about it Chandler; was she there?"

Chandler saw three sets of eyes boring into him; Martin's, Rush's, and Cal Given's. He slumped back on the sofa. "Leave her out of it," he mumbled.

Frank swung towards Rush. "Was she there?"

"Sure she was there, only it wasn't planned out at the ranch. It was planned right here in this room, and Belle served us coffee and listened in. She even said hanging him in the barn doorway was a good idea; that it'd put the fear of God into the other small ranchers."

George Harrison's face was white, his strong jaw clamped down and his eyes ice-like in their staring stillness. He moved past Ken Martin towards the sofa. Frank's sharp tone halted him.

"George!"

"Get it over with," the older man said thickly. "You've heard enough, Frank. We all have."

Frank drew back a long breath and exhaled it. In the absolute stillness everyone in the room heard air sweep into his lungs and out again. "Untie Rush," he said to George, "and Ken Martin."

As George moved to obey badly frightened Cal Given looked past him imploringly. "Not me," he whispered to Frank. "I helped you, Harrison. I told you everything you wanted to know. Not me . . ."

"They're loose, Frank."

Charley Bemis backed away holding his riot-gun high in both hands. "They're the worst two," he said, never taking his eyes

194

off the released men. "You hadn't ought to turn 'em loose."

Frank watched Sam Rush flex his arms. He knew what he had to do and it sickened him. He had known dozens of range riders like Rush; men who feared neither man nor devil but who would kill as readily in a face-to-face shoot-out as they would also kill from ambush. Men without principles; without, actually, any actual comprehension of what was right and what was wrong. And yet they were brave and loyal men.

"Gimme a gun," Rush said, no fear showing in his face at all. "Like your brother says – let's get it over with."

Before Frank moved several things occurred simultaneously. From the east wall came Will's quick roll of knuckles warning everyone in the room of more Rafter C men coming. Luke Chandler heaved upright and stood large in the smoky lamplight. "Don't give him a gun," he shot at Frank. "He won't use it on you, not now."

Sam Rush made a slow smile at his employer; an enigmatic smile that needed no words. Then Belle moved; jumped up to stand so close to her brother their arms were together. She was breathing heavily. One of the tied men groaned and rolled over trying to shake his head clear. Frank's attention was momentarily distracted by this sound and a sudden explosion burst out.

Charley Bemis let off an involuntary scream and pulled both triggers of his riot-gun. It was aimed fully at Ken Martin from a distance of less than fifteen feet. The range-boss was knocked off his feet by the blast and instantly killed. Frank was dropping to the floor and streaking for his gun when the second shot came, and with it a blur of movement as Luther Chandler hurled himself towards a window. George fired instinctively and missed. Chandler collided with Sam Rush, was staggered, and in that second Frank saw the little nickel plated double-barrelled .41 calibre derringer in his hand. Another blast erupted from George's gun and Chandler shuddered.

Sam Rush, knocked back against the window by Chandler's momentum twisted wildly and threw himself against the glass. In a flash he was gone into the night.

Outside there was a loud cry of alarm and two sudden crashing pistol shots, a period of sudden shocked stillness, then four mingling shots, and finally silence.

George Harrison lunged towards the window and stumbled over Cal Given who had dropped like a stone at the first shot. George lost his gun, hit the floor on all fours, swore and groped along the carpet for his carbine then got up with a fierce snarl at Cal Given.

Only Belle had not moved. As Frank came slowly upright he caught her gaze and held it. "Good work," he said. "Where did you have it hidden?"

"Where you wouldn't have dared look for it!" she snarled and moved to where Luther was sitting with his back to the wall looking wide-eyed at a spreading stain on his coat-front. As Belle knelt Luther looked up out of dry, misting eyes, then he bent forward in the middle and hung there a second before tilting away and gliding out his full length, dead.

Will burst past the front door with his cocked short-gun swinging. He saw George peering out the window and called forward. "George; are you hurt?"

The elder Harrison turned, his face was fierce and his eyes fire-like. "No, I'm not hurt. Rush got away. We got to get him."

Frank reached over and pushed Will's gun-hand down. He seemed the least excited in the room. "Chandler and Martin are dead, Will. Let's do like George says."

They started for the door. George jerked

suddenly upright. "Bemis," he said to the re-loading younger man. "You stay here and . . ."

"You stay with him," Frank said from the doorway. When George moved to protest Frank nodded towards the tied men. "There are still some others you know; he came to town with eight men. By now everyone in Pioche heard the shooting and knows there was a fight. That means the Rafter C might come down here lookin' for Chandler. Put out that light and wait here for 'em with Bemis, George."

He and Will passed out into the darkness, skirted the side of the house and stood in the chill, listening. Overhead clouds were breaking up, drifting away to reveal sharp, bright stars and a milky moon. "Here," Will said, pointing. "That's where he landed. Yonder – there go his tracks." Will looked around. "He's unarmed isn't he?"

"Yes. Will?"

"Yeah?"

"What happened outside?"

Will showed impatience. "Couple Rafter C boys came down the road. 'Bout then hell busted loose inside. They stopped a second then started for the house in a run with their guns out. I let 'em get almost to the picket-gate then I dumped one with a shot in the leg. The other one tried for my gun-flash. He missed and I didn't. The last I saw of 'em the last one was dragging the first one back up the road with his good arm." Will inched along studying Sam Rush's tracks in the mud. "They'll live but won't either of 'em go bear hunting or anything like that for a while. Come on, Frank; he's cuttin' around behind the house like maybe he wants to get back uptown."

They tracked Sam Rush through a number of rear yards. Here and there lights flickered to life in the homes they passed. Once a large dog hurled himself at Will, a chain sang taut and the dog was brought up short, still straining. Will eyed the slavering beast and told Frank he hoped that chain held.

They broke out into the alley behind Pioche's livery barn, but there it was hard to follow Rush's trail. Frank moved past, entered the barn from the rear and went along its broad corridor towards a motionless silhouette up near the front. The nighthawk turned with a start, saw the badge Frank forgot he wore still, and made an audible sigh.

"What's goin' on, Marshal? 'Feller come

through here a minute ago like Old Nick was after him."

"Did you recognise him?"

"Well; I know he was a Chandler-man 'cause I've seen him before, but I don't know his name or nothin' like that."

"Where did he go?"

"Straight across the road towards the cattlemen's saloon – then down to the hotel."

"Thanks. Come on, Will."

"Marshal?"

"Yes?"

"He took my pistol."

Pioche's main thoroughfare was dark except for the twin coach lanterns on either side of the hotel's entrance. Frank stopped in the darkness and threw up an arm to restrain his brother. Opposite them were the dark windows of the hotel's second floor rooms.

"He's had time to get ready, Will. You make a run for it a minute or so after I'm gone."

"What's the sense in splitting up?" Will demanded.

"There's a back entrance. I'm going around there. You go in the front way. We'll meet in the hallway." Frank rolled up on the balls of his feet and balanced there, watching the hotel windows. Beside him Will muttered. "Why didn't he swipe a horse from the barn and run for it?"

"Didn't think he had the time," retorted Frank, and lunged forward out into the moonlight. He got half across the road when a crashing gunshot flung up a gout of mud three feet behind him. He heard Will bellow in astonishment and a moment later thumb off a shot. Then Frank was across the way heading for the dog-trot which would take him into the back-lots. Behind him there was a brief and furious hand-gun duel then silence. Frank smiled; Will had made Rush empty his gun before he too made the crossing.

There were a number of dogs barking excitedly now, out in the night, and Frank knew, as he went along towards the hotel's rear doorway, that there also were a number of awakened people sitting up in bed listening, waiting, wondering.

He got inside and was immediately swallowed by a darkness deeper than night, felt along the wall until he located the stair-well and began an inch by inch ascent. There was not a sound; stillness dripped and eddied.

When the landing came he almost missed it, brought his foot down hard expecting still one more step. The sound carried quiveringly forward and Frank halted, near holding his breath.

A voice came out to him. "Harrison?"

He remained stone-like, placing the sound.

"Harrison? Oh hell; let's don't play games. Come on – I'm waitin' for you."

From the opposite end of the hallway came Will's answer. "Come on out, Rush."

For just a second there was no answer, then: "Two of you, huh? Well; all right. Come on. I won't go alone I'll tell you that."

"Rush," called out Frank, "we'll give you a fair chance. Come out."

The Rafter C man laughed. It was a thin and tinny sound that grated along Frank's nerves. "Yeah; I know the kind of chance you'll give me. Like I give your brother – a slug in the back o' the head." The voice faded, then swelled again. "Come on, boys; let's see who can shoot best in the dark."

Frank edged out into the hallway. He had placed Rush and began a steady advance towards the open door of his room. Will too moved out into sight and edged along the wall. They were converging. From within his room Sam Rush heard boards whine underfoot and turn silent when his stalkers paused. He lifted the liveryman's gun and aimed it outward, waiting, but when leaden moments passed with no more sounds he called loudly: "Hey, Harrison – you with the badge on. Tell you what: you come up where I can see you and we'll shoot it out."

Before Frank answered Will said dryly, "Sure, Rush; Frank'd trust you like he'd trust a nest of rattlers."

Frank punched three bullets from his shell-belt, worked them loosely in his fist and motioned with his head for Will to remain where he was. Then he dropped belly-down and worked forward to the edge of Rush's doorway. He tossed all three bullets inside the room and brought up his gun-hand. Rush fired at the sounds, blue-burning powder lanced into the night and the hotel roared with the explosion. Frank thumbed off two quick shots at Rush's muzzle-blast. He got back a second, third, and fourth shots. Then he fired three times and through the heart of the thunder he heard Rush let off a high cry, then the echoes raced away with Rush's fading voice and there was only the strong swirl of gunpowder left.

Over a terrible silence came the bubbling, guttering breathing of a man. Frank got to his feet, re-loaded methodically and looked up. Will was watching him, his gun pointing upwards, balancing there in one big fist. "You got him," Will said quietly, and they both entered the room, Will bringing his gun to bear on the faintly stirring dark lump back against the east wall, waiting to put in the final shot. Sam Rush groaned. "Darker'n hell," he muttered. Will went in search of a lamp. "That you, Harrison?"

"It's me, Rush."

"Well – there wasn't no other way, was there?"

"No there wasn't."

Will found and lit a lamp. He came back walking with unconscious softness. "Dead?" he asked Frank. The older brother made a faint negative head-shake; he could still hear the faint-growing breathing.

"Want a drink, Rush?"

"Naw; I guess not. Harrison? Where is it?"

Frank flicked a glance at the fatal wounds showing glistening black under Will's high-held lamp. "Lungs," he said, and did not say there were three wounds within the spacing of a man's hand, all fatal.

The breathing stopped. Will bent a little, listening. "Rush?"

Frank brushed past going out of the room. "Come on," he said from the hallway. "Leave the lamp there."

Outside, dawn was coming over a cloudless sky. They stood together watching first light break glassily into the hush with a long, pale streak of pink light. There was an edge of coldness, a briskness, to this new day. There was also a promise, something never-ending, that went into Frank and winnowed away some of the turmoil. A voice rose and held strongly in the dawn stillness from the marshal's office down the road.

"Frank! Will! Over here. Charley and I've got 'em all locked up over here."

Frank did not move at once and Will said under his breath, "This might be trouble." He was looking north along the plankwalk where a group of men were coming towards them.

Frank recognised the medical man Ambrose Pierce. He turned, waiting, with Will beside him. The doctor peered a moment at Will with obvious interest then said, "There's a rumour afloat that Luther Chandler is dead."

"It's true," Frank agreed. "There's another Rafter C man upstairs in the hotel dead. His name is Sam Rush. Over at Belle Chandler's house Ken Martin is also dead."

The men with Pierce were solemn-faced and silent. Their gazes flickered over Frank; from his slack, grey and tired face to the badge on his shirt-front, and up to his greeny eyes. One of them said, "Did Chandler appoint you Town Marshal?"

Frank remembered the badge and removed it without replying. He gave it to Doctor Pierce still without speaking. "Anything else?" he asked finally.

The doctor looked at his companions. They were all staring at the Harrison brothers. "No," he said, "I guess not right now."

Frank and Will crossed through the muddy roadway bound for Pioche's jailhouse. They were met by George and Charley Bemis. "Got 'em all under lock but the dead ones," George said, gazing into Frank's face. "How about Rush?"

"He's dead at the hotel."

George looked up the roadway. It was turning pleasantly bright now with new sunshine, and steam arose from beyond the plankwalk. "That big-gutted fellow with the doctor you were talking to was the mayor," George said absently. "He's also an attorney here in Pioche."

Frank went inside and stopped. The strap-steel cell was full and every face was turned towards him. "Let 'em all out but Given, Belle, and that young feller there," he said to Will.

Will hesitated and George came quickly forward. "You can't do that, Frank. They're Chandler's men."

Frank jerked his head at Will. "Let 'em out," he repeated, and said no more until the Rafter C riders were milling in the centre of the room. "I reckon you boys know what this was all about by now, don't you?"

"Yes sir," a swarthy, black-eyed man said.

"And it's all over now. Chandler, Carson, Rush and Ken Martin are dead."

"Yes," the same man exclaimed.

"Well; any of you want to take it up for them?"

There was a quick murmur of dissent and a shuffling of booted feet. Frank waited until silence returned.

"Then get on your horses and slope," he said. "Be out of Pioche by high noon – all of you. If you aren't . . ."

"We will be," the dark man interrupted to say quickly. "Even the hurt ones."

Frank gestured towards the open door. "Go on." As the cowboys shouldered through the doorway he looked at young Bent Rodger who was leaning against the bars staring at him. "How about you?" he asked.

"I'll go, Mister Harrison. I never wanted to do anything but wrangle horses for Chandler."

"But I owe you something for telling Chandler about me," Frank said.

Rodger protested immediately. "I was working for him. What'd you expect me to do?"

Will nodded approval. "That's right, Frank. A man's loyal to his outfit."

Frank went to a chair and sank down. "Go on," he said to Rodger. "Will; turn him out too."

George was heating some coffee. He turned now wearing a frown. "Maybe the people here in Pioche'll want to try those men," he said.

Frank, feeling burnt out and useless,

spoke quietly. "I'm the law here, George, until someone supersedes me, and I say they haven't committed any crime." He made a wry face. "They never got the chance to. Go on, Rodger. Saddle up and leave the country."

George waited, watching Frank. Will too, was waiting. Only Cal Given and Belle Chandler remained in the cell, both stony-silent.

"Given?"

"Yes."

"You've got to answer to the Town Council."

"But I didn't do anything."

"Maybe that's the crime they'll charge you with." George brought Frank a cup of coffee. "Belle?"

"Yes."

He rummaged for words and found none suitable. Her dark gaze held him pinioned. He saw her stilled face, the sag of her shoulders, the shining of her hair and he remembered the great wave of warmth that had come to him from her lips. He got up suddenly and took the cup of coffee to the doorway; stood there gazing up the roadway.

"Better get our horses," he said over his

shoulder to Will. "It's a long way from here to – someplace else."

As Will moved to press past and leave the office George spoke. "Frank; this is a good place. It's a thriving town and the range is as good as anything back in Colorado. A drifter could put down roots here."

The coffee was bitter but Frank downed it and returned to the table to set it down. "No," he said. "Jess is here, George. Jess and something else – another part of me that died here." He raised his eyes and looked squarely into Belle Chandler's face. After a moment she bit her lip and whirled away from him facing the wall. There was a scalding mistiness obscuring her vision.

"I'll ride on, George. You and Will go back to your jobs and one of these days we'll meet again."

He smiled then, affectionately at the older man, and left the room. A little later Will entered the office and looked soberly at the older man. "He just got astride and rode off, George. Just said s'long and rode off."

"Yeah, Will, I know. But he'll stop pretty soon now. Frank got a big drink of life here in Pioche; he got a big enough dose to age him, and when a man gets old in the head he settles down. I think Frank's ridden his last trail as a drifter." George cleared his throat. "Here; have some coffee; quit brooding, kid. Life is like that – before anyone gets to be a man he's got to go through a certain amount of tempering."

From the cell a voice came softly, the words spoken swiftly in order to be steady. "What about a woman, Mister Harrison?"

Both George and Will looked up. "I guess that applies to women too," George said, feeling compassion. "Why did you let them kill Jess?"

"I didn't. That was an outright lie, what Sam Rush said and he knew it, but he hated Luther so badly he tried to soil me too. Before God I swear to you I did not know they were even planning to run your brother out of Meadow Valley."

"You could have told Frank that," Will said, knowing she was speaking the truth.

"No I couldn't have. He killed Rush believing *him*. He would never have believed me."

George looked at the coffee cup in his hand and thought this was true, but even if it was not true, Belle Chandler and Frank could never have had anything between them. Jess would always have been there to keep them apart. He looked up when a man's voice came into the room from the doorway.

"Gentlemen?"

Will turned fully towards the newcomers. "Well?" he said warily.

"Gentlemen; I'm the mayor and this is the Town Council, and this I think you know is Doctor Ambrose Pierce." The townsmen came closer and stopped. Doctor Pierce was searching the room.

"Where is your brother?" he asked.

"Gone. He rode out a little while ago."

"But he'll be back won't he?"

"No."

Pierce was nonplussed. "But we wanted to hire him as Town Marshal."

Will and George exchanged a look and only Will was amused. "Sorry," he said. "Now, if that's all you fellers have to say – come on, George."

"But, gentlemen . . ."

The remaining two Harrison brothers struck out for the hotel without a backward glance, outward bound from Pioche in Meadow Valley.